Silent Screams

SAMANTHA MICHAELS

First and foremost, I need to thank my husband and our dog. I'd be lost without you.

* * *

To the amazing team at Carxander Publishing, thank you for keeping me as sane as possible.

* * *

A special shout-out to Caitlin Loggins and Maryann Beatty for going above and beyond sharing my work.

* * *

Most importantly, to the readers who've taken a chance on my crazy stories - THANK YOU!!

Chapter One

Mel

"Well, that was eventful," Jason, or Jay as his friends call him, says when he pops into my office the day after Memorial Day.

"You can say that again," I say, unable to get the picture of Daniel flat on his back out of my head. If he hadn't come to our home with my idiot sister, Judd wouldn't have had to deck him.

"Seen Daniel today?"

"Not yet, but I'm expecting I will."

"Promise me you won't take any crap. Technically, he was trespassing."

"Good point, but not sure it will matter."

"I gotta run, early vendor call, but I got your back. Lunch today?"

"Assuming I'm still employed here, sure."

Jay waves as he walks away. I open my email and see a meeting request from my former assistant turned Human Resources intern, Allie. My nerves kick in, and I'm grateful the meeting is scheduled for ten, so I don't have to sweat it all day. I head down a little before ten, and Allie takes me into Carla's, the HR director's, office.

"Can I get you anything?" Allie asks.

"Coffee, please," I respond.

She hands me the cup and says, "Carla will be here shortly."

I'm seated in the chair in front of Carla's desk while Allie sits at the small table next to the desk. A few minutes after ten, Carla walks in, so I stand. After a brief handshake, she walks to her side of the desk and sits.

"Please, have a seat," Carla says, her tone serious. "Ms. McNeill, I'd like to discuss the complaint you filed against Mr. Daniel O'Laughlin."

"Okay."

"We take these complaints seriously, but we're concerned that Mr. Walker took things into his own hands."

"I beg your pardon. One had nothing to do with the other."

"Mr O'Laughlin tells a different story."

Anger fills my stomach, so I take a deep breath and exhale slowly. "And may I ask what?"

"He claims Mr. Walker got physical defending you."

"That's true, but not for what happened at work. Rather, it was due to something he said to me that night."

"Do you have proof?"

"Do I need it? How can what happened in the privacy of my property carry consequences here?"

"It can when the other party is a relative of the owner."

"So, there are different rules?"

"No, but he is the owner's nephew."

"I understand that, but I don't understand why that matters. The incident didn't occur on company property or at a company sponsored event."

"Understand we aren't planning to take any action at this time."

"Then why am I in here?"

"Because we're dropping your complaint against him."

"But that happened here." I feel my blood boil as I think about him making all of those sexist remarks and revealing my salary to my sister.

Carla ignores my last statement and instead says, "That's all for today, Ms. McNeill. Please keep this discussion confidential."

My legs feel like jelly when I stand, and I barely make it out of Carla's office. I can hear Allie calling my name, but I ignore her and speed-walk to my office, shutting and locking the door behind me. I manage to compose myself by lunchtime, greeting Jay with a smile when I stop by his office.

"You okay?"

"Yeah, why would you ask?"

"You seem off, girl."

"I'm fine."

"I know you better than that. Come on, Mel, talk to me."

"Really, Jay, all good. I promise."

"Well, I'm always here."

"I know."

Just as I reach my office after lunch, I hear the last voice I want to hear.

"Did you enjoy your morning?" Daniel asks.

"Like any other," I respond with a shrug.

"Oh? So, you're questioned by HR every day?"

"I don't know what you're talking about."

"Oh, come on. Yes you do. Nothing to say in response?"

"Again, I don't know what you're referring to. Is there anything else you need, or can I get back to work?"

With a smirk, he says, "I'll catch you later."

Mercifully, the rest of the day goes quickly. I sneak out and race home, wanting nothing except to see Judd and our girls.

I smell the grill when I pull into the driveway, so I head out back. Our furry-girls, Daisy and Lily, are busy chasing squirrels while Judd stands at the grill. The food smells like heaven, but it's the man cooking it that makes my mouth water.

"Oh my god, when did you get that?" I exclaim.

Judd's standing there wearing an apron that says *"Once You Put My Meat In Your Mouth, You're Going To Want More."*

"Found it online. You like it?"

"Yeah." I try to laugh, but I'm still upset.

"That's it? Yeah? I thought you would love it."

"I'm sorry. I do love it."

"You okay?"

"Just tired." I give him a small smile.

Yeah, tired of dealing with Daniel.

Thankfully, he seems to buy the half-lie. "Okay, sweetie. Good news is dinner's almost ready."

"Thank you. Let me just run in and change."

I throw on a one-piece swimsuit under a tee shirt and cut-off denim shorts. When I come back down, two plates and two glasses of wine are waiting for me out by the garden. The air around me is filled with barbecue chicken with roasted potatoes, and accompanied by Italian dressing on a spinach, tomato, and fresh mozzarella salad. Everything looks and smells delicious, but I can barely bring myself to take a bite.

"Baby, are you sure you're okay?" Leave it to Judd to notice.

"Yeah."

"You're quiet."

"Tired."

Judd looks at me but doesn't say anything, pretty much how we spend the rest of the meal. I almost spill my guts a couple of times, but this is my issue to deal with, not his.

After we clean up, we head back outside.

"How about a soak in the hot tub?" Judd asks.

"I was planning on it," I say as I reveal my swimsuit.

"You don't need that swimsuit."

"Oh, sorry," I say, lowering my head. I thought he liked the way I looked, but I guess I make him sick, too. Story of my life.

"Baby, I was teasing."

"Oh." But I'm not so sure.

Leaving my suit on, I climb into the tub and wait for Judd. He turns the jets on, and I feel my stress finally dissipate.

I steal a glance at my sexy cowboy and tears prick my eyes. Shit, I can't cry in front of him. I don't want him worrying about me. I splash my face then wipe my eyes. Since we stayed dressed, Judd left the door open to the hot tub room.

"Hey, lovebirds," I hear Lexi call over the fence.

"Hey," I say as Lexi and Damien head over. "What's up?"

"Any plans this weekend?" Lexi asks.

"I don't think so," I say, looking at Judd.

"Nothing specific," Judd says.

"Good, then I'm stealing this one," Lexi says, pointing at me.

"Oh? For what?" I ask.

"A girls glamping weekend."

"Oh. Are you sure you want me to come?" I ask.

"Why wouldn't I?"

"Well, after the group outing to celebrate Judd and I getting together, then when you said I'm boring, I wasn't sure."

I stare at Lexi as she processes what I just said. Her face turns red. Good. She hurt me, and she should be embarrassed. The group dinner to celebrate Judd and me was her idea, yet she ignored me the entire time.

"Look, I know what I did and said were wrong, and I'm so sorry. I don't have an excuse. I was just having a tough time, and I took it out on you."

"I understand, but please, next time, talk to me instead."

"I promise. So, you coming?" Lexi asks.

"I appreciate the invite, but you should have fun with your friends."

"But, you're my best friend. I want you there."

Fighting a sigh, I say, "Okay."

All I want is some peace and quiet this weekend. Instead, I have to deal with a group of loud women. I love Lexi, but since she became friends with the wives of the band Stardust, Alex, Hannah, Eden, and Lizzie, she's become loud like them. But, it's only a weekend. I can handle it.

"Great. Alex is driving, so she'll pick us both up here."

"I'll be ready."

Chapter Two

Mel

I duck out of work early on Friday so I can be ready for the weekend. I wish I was more excited, but I really would rather stay home with Judd and the girls. I walk over to Lexi's and wait for Alex.

I spend most of the ride to the house we'll be staying the weekend at gazing out the window, only speaking when addressed.

When we arrive, I see the house. It's impressive. The outside looks like a simple log cabin, but inside is a whole other story. Though there's only one floor, there's a ton of space. The lilac walls feature white and yellow daisies. The house features six bedrooms, each painted a different pastel color and home to a queen-sized bed.

There's also a kitchen, living room, dining area, and a game room with a hot tub, along with two full bathrooms. No part of the house makes me smile more than the individual bedrooms. I stand by and let the others pick their rooms, taking what's left. I'd be perfectly happy just sitting in here and reading dirty romance novels all weekend. But no, the chatty crew is bouncing around like they each ate a pound of sugar.

"There's a great bar about thirty minutes from here," Alex says.

I sit down on the couch and watch the sugar sisters scurrying around and getting ready.

"You're not changing?" Lexi asks as she sits down next to me.

"I'm fine like this."

"But there might be hot men there."

"And?"

"Don't you wanna make a good impression?"

"Couldn't care less. I have Judd."

The other girls emerge, so we head out. When we get to the bar, there's a table reserved for us. Alex orders two bottles of wine and two bottles of champagne for the table.

"Can I also get a glass of water, please?" I ask our waitress.

She brings our drinks and takes our food order.

"Time to hit the dance floor," Lexi says.

"I'll wait for the food and keep an eye on everyone's bag," I say.

I grab the book I tucked away in my bag and start reading when, suddenly, I'm interrupted by a male voice.

"What's a pretty lady like you doing by yourself?"

"I'm not by myself. My friends are dancing."

"Well, you should be, too. Care to join me?"

"No, thank you."

"Oh come on, don't be a tease."

"Uh, you approached me. I was sitting here minding my own business."

"Oh, now we've moved on to bitch, huh?"

I glare. "Don't call me a bitch. You don't even know me."

He grabs my arm and tries to pull me up.

"Get your damn hands off of me!" I shout.

Before I realize what's happening, I feel his hands leave my arm as he falls to the floor. Looking up, I see one of the bouncers pick him up, throw him over his shoulder, and throw him out the front door.

"Are you okay, miss?" the bouncer asks when he returns to our table.

"Yes, thank you," I say.

My face heats up as I notice everyone staring at me. Great. I just made an ass out of myself. I would give anything to be teleported home.

I stick with water while the rest of them polish off drink after drink. When they return to the dance floor, I take Alex's keys out of her purse.

Once the DJ announces last call, I gather up everyone's bags and the bouncers help me get the drunky sisters out to the car. I drive back to the cabin and manage to get them all inside.

The following morning, I'm the first one up, so I start a pot of coffee. While that brews, I cook up a pound of bacon and make French toast. One by one, five scary monsters emerge from their sleeping quarters. Their faces feature various colors of smudged makeup, and good lord, the hair. Each of them shuffles to the dining area and plops down in a chair. I grab my phone and snap a picture.

As soon as everything's ready, I give a plate and a cup of coffee to each of them, chuckling as all I hear are groans from the Sloshed Sister Society. After they finish, I clean up as they each head off to get cleaned up. I take my book and go sit out back. The peace and quiet remind me of the home Judd bought us. I feel a lump in my throat thinking about him. I miss him so much. I'd rather be home with him.

I hear the girls gathering in the living room.

"How about another bar tonight?" Alex asks.

Oh great, here we go again.

"Sounds good," Hannah says.

The rest of the girls agree. When it's time to head out, I grab another book and trudge out to Alex's car. As we enter the bar, I see a sign for a poker tournament happening that night. We head to a table, and when a waitress stops by, we order food and wine for the table. When the waitress brings the wine, Lexi pours six glasses, handing one to each of us.

"Time to hit the dance floor," Lexi says. I'm not up for dancing, so I pass.

I watch as they all put their bags on and head out to the dance floor. I walk to the bar to grab a soda, and while I'm waiting, I look at the sign for the poker tournament and decide to sign up. The bartender gives me my soda and points me to the room where the tourney is being held.

"Welcome to the tournament. I'm your host, Tommy," someone says to me when I enter.

"Thanks."

"You're the only woman signed up. Best of luck. Just give your entrance fee to Carla at the table over there," he says as he nods in her direction, "and she'll give you your chips."

I hit the ATM and grab the thousand dollar entrance fee, then head over and hand it to Carla.

"Best of luck to you, Mel. Show these men how it's done!"

"I'll try my best," I say, smiling for the first time this weekend. Taking my chip tray, I sit down at one of the tables, and all seven of my opponents look at me with amusement on their faces. *Go ahead, underestimate me.*

Once all the seats are filled, Tommy grabs a microphone. "Welcome everyone. For tonight's tourney, we have eight tables of eight players. Each table will play until one person remains. Those eight players will battle it out at our final table. Tonight's prize is twenty-five thousand. Now, let's shuffle up and deal."

The man sitting across from me asks, "Do you need us to explain the rules before we start?"

While seething on the inside, I smile and respond, "I'll figure it out as I go."

One by one, I pick off my opponents until it's just me and the condescending dickhead from earlier. He flashes me the cockiest smile I've ever seen.

I spend the next thirty minutes wiping it off him, winning all but one hand, the knockout blow coming when two aces appear in the flop.

Dickhead and his pocket kings thought he had me, and shoved all-in. Imagine his shock when I called and flipped over pocket aces!

Once all the other tables were done, the eight of us winners gathered at the final table. I couldn't help noticing that the men were treating me differently this time around.

The final table begins after a short break. Within half an hour, we're down to four players. I'm currently second in chips, only one thousand less than the first place player. Word spreads, and a din fills the room as more spectators join the crowd. After an hour, I'm in the final two, about five thousand chips out of first place.

"We're down to our final two players," Tommy announces. "Currently in second place, we have newcomer, Mel McNeill, and in first place, we have ten-time champion, Jake Taylor. Best of luck to both competitors."

Jake and I sit at opposite ends of the table. I want nothing more than to slap the smirk off his face, but I take a deep breath and prepare myself to play.

After about an hour of trading the chip lead back and forth, I'm dealt an ace and ten of hearts. I'm the big blind, and Jake is small blind.

He calls, and I check. The dealer lays down the flop, and it takes every ounce of restraint not to get up and dance.

"All in," Jake announces.

Jake has me covered with a ten thousand chip lead. I call, putting myself all in, and a smug smile crosses his face.

In about five seconds, that smile will be gone, asshole.

With a small shimmy, Jake flips his cards. Ace of diamonds, ten of spades.

"With a king, queen and jack of hearts on the table, that's an ace high straight for Jake," Tommy announces. "Mel's gonna need a miracle."

With a loud sigh, I flip my cards and a chorus of gasps fills the room.

"Holy shit," Tommy exclaims. "Mel has an ace and ten of hearts, giving her a royal flush."

"With that sigh, I thought I had you. Good hand," Jake says.

"Thank you," I say.

Jake is left with only ten thousand chips, which he shoves all in on the next hand. He turns over a pair of kings while I have an eight and a queen of diamonds.

One diamond and two spades come up on the flop, followed by another diamond on the turn. The only way Jake can lose is a fifth diamond on the river.

And when that diamond appears, I let out a small squeal as I stand.

After I'm announced the winner, I walk over to Jake and shake his hand.

"Congratulations," Jake says.

"Thank you. You were a tough opponent."

"Thanks to all our players for a great tourney. And congratulations to our winner," Tommy announces. As the room clears out, Tommy walks over to me. "All that's left is to settle your prize," he says, taking a book out of his briefcase. He hands me a check for the prize money, which I quickly tuck into my purse.

"One of our bouncers will escort you to your car when you're ready to head out."

"Thanks again. This was a blast."

When I walk out to the main bar, I see the girls sitting at our table, so I walk over.

"Where were you?" Lexi asks.

"I went to the poker tournament."

"We heard some woman, playing her first tourney here, knocked off a champ," Alex says.

Smiling, I reply, "I sure as hell did."

"Wow," Lexi says, her eyes wide. "When did you learn how to play?"

"Judd's been teaching me."

"That's awesome, girl," Hannah says.

As we're sitting there, Tommy walks over carrying a tray with six champagne glasses. "Thought you'd want to toast your friend," he says as he passes out the glasses.

The girls raise their glasses, and I feel my cheeks catch fire. Eden says, "To Mel," as she raises her glass. Everyone follows suit. We all clink glasses and down our drinks.

"What do you say we head out?" Alex asks.

"Keys, please," I say, holding out my hand.

I stop at the bar on the way out, and Tommy grabs one of the bouncers to walk us out. Once we've pulled out of the lot, he goes back inside. When we get back to the house, the drunk divas all head to bed. Once I'm in my room, I text Judd.

You up?

Yeah, he texts back right away, like he was just waiting to hear from me.

Mind if I call?

Of course not.

I call right away.

"Hey, beautiful," Judd says when he answers.

"Mmm, hey, sexy."

"What's up?"

"I have big news. We went to a bar tonight, and I won a poker tourney."

"Oh my god, baby, that's amazing!"

"It's all thanks to you teaching me."

"All those fun nights of strip poker."

"Yeah." My cheeks flush. I have a check for twenty-five grand in my purse."

"Damn, woman. I'm so proud of you. We're gonna need to get you a poker name."

"Yeah, like my favorite player, Vanessa Rousso. I need something cool like her Lady Maverick title."

"I can't wait until you get home tomorrow."

"Oh yeah?"

"I miss your warm body next to me in bed."

I blush an even deeper shade of red. "I miss you, too. But for now, I need to get some sleep." I hate that it's without him.

"Me too. Good night, baby. I love you."

"Good night, my sexy cowboy. I love you more.

Chapter Three

Mel

Judd and the girls are sitting on the porch when Alex pulls into the driveway. I feel my mouth water at the mere sight of my man. Okay, truth, more than just my mouth was watering.

I practically run to the porch, where I'm greeted by two wiggly butts and a sexy man literally sweeping me off my feet. As I'm twirling through the air, I feel a sense of peace and calm wash over me.

"Wow, that's one heck of a greeting," I say.

"Nothing but the best for my girl."

"Oh, I didn't mean yours. I meant theirs," I tease, nodding toward our dogs.

"Meanie," Judd says, sticking his tongue out at me.

"Ooh, I know where you can put that," I purr.

"Patience, my love. Right now, I'm taking you out to dinner to celebrate the new poker queen. Where would you like to go?"

"Palermo's. It's my favorite."

"You got it, doll."

Before we pull out of our driveway, Judd puts *The Gambler* by

Kenny Rogers on the radio. We sing it at the top of our lungs as we drive to Palermo's.

When we get inside, we're seated at our favorite booth in the back corner of the restaurant. Judd orders a bottle of Moscato. He pours two glasses and hands me one.

"A toast to my queen," he says, his glass in the air.

"Thank you, my king." We clink glasses and each take a sip.

I down my entire plate of chicken fettuccine alfredo while Judd polishes off chicken Parmesan over ziti.

After dinner, we pick up the girls and head to the dog park. We play with the dogs until they're both exhausted then head back home. The sun starts its descent as we sit by the garden holding hands, both dogs curled up at our feet.

"This, right here, is perfect," Judd says.

"You're perfect."

"Not even close, but with you, I'm the best man I can be."

"You're perfect for me."

"We were made for each other, my love."

"Awww, you're such a cinnamon roll."

"A what?" he asks with a confused furrowed eyebrow.

"A cinnamon roll."

He shakes his head with an amused grin. "You lost me, babe."

"You know how I love all those spicy romance novels? Well, when the male lead is sweet outside of the bedroom, he's referred to as a cinnamon roll. There's even an awesome group I joined on social media celebrating that type of character."

"Hmmm." His grin becomes wicked. "Maybe you'd like a taste of my icing when we get inside."

"Damn, right, cowboy! Let's go!"

I take off into the house, and right to the bedroom. I'm already half-naked when Judd gets inside. He grabs me, throws me on the bed, and rocks my world.

I lay in my cowboys arms after one hell of a screamfest.

"I wish I'd been there to see you play."

"Me too. You woulda been proud."

"I'm always proud of my girl."

14

"Well, you may change your mind."

"And why is that?"

"I'm not sure I wanna stay at O'Laughlin," I blurt after taking a deep breath.

"Daniel?"

"Yeah, in part. But, I'm also not sure I wanna be stuck in an office anymore."

"So, what would you wanna do instead?"

"What do you think about maybe expanding what we do and start making meals? Like, we could get a booth at the farmer's market for not only our produce, but meals that people could just heat up. And, the meals would be affordable for everyone."

"I love the idea. But are you sure?"

"Well, I'm not ready to go quit just yet, but yeah, I'm leaning that way."

"Just promise me we'll talk about it before you do anything."

"Of course. I realize it'll be a big change. I was also thinking, we could start a separate account with my winnings to put aside in case we do decide to do it."

"Okay. I'm going to follow you to the bank in the morning. I'll feel better if you're not going in alone with that much money."

"Always the protector, huh?"

"For you, always, my love."

The next morning, after we finished up at the bank, I head to work while Judd goes back home. I get to work about half an hour later than usual, but Mr. O'Laughlin has never held us to a specific schedule, a perk of the position. Apparently, his nephew didn't get the memo.

"Nice of you to finally show up," Daniel says, as he stands in the doorway of my office.

"I beg your pardon?"

"Must be nice to just wander in whenever you want."

"Your uncle has never held us to a specific schedule. I had some business to handle this morning, so I came in a little later than usual. I also work more than forty hours most weeks, so that has never been an issue."

"Well, it is now. Don't let it happen again."

"With all due respect, Daniel, your uncle is my boss, not you."

"Well, we'll just have to see about that."

Daniel turns on his heel and storms out, not giving me a chance to respond. I take a deep breath, count to twenty, and get to work. Noon rolls around, and Jason stops by.

"Lunch?"

I shake my head. "Nah, just gonna eat here."

"Everything okay?" His voice is laced with concern.

"I had an errand and came in a little later, so just trying to catch up."

"I could join you here. I just need to grab food. Anything you need to go with yours?"

"I didn't bring anything, but please don't worry. I'm good."

He doesn't look convinced. "If you change your mind, you know where to find me."

I smile and nod. Jason heads out.

About fifteen minutes later, he reappears with two sandwiches and two bottles of water. This time, my smile is genuine, grateful to have such a good friend.

"Got you a BLT on rye."

"You're the best. Thank you."

"I am, aren't I?"

Jason sits down in the chair on the other side of my desk, and we both open our sandwiches.

"So, do anything fun this weekend?" he asks.

"Actually, yeah." I fill him on the poker tourney. "That's why I was late this morning. Judd and I went to the bank to deposit my winnings."

"Damn, girl, that's awesome."

"Judd's been teaching me."

"I bet he has." The sarcasm drips from his voice as he waggles his eyebrows with a grin.

"Shut it, asshole!"

"Hey! I got you lunch."

We both laugh, hoping that Daniel doesn't make a surprise appearance. We stifle our laughter just in case.

After we're done eating, Jason heads back to his office while I finish my day working on expense reports.

When I get home, the dogs are in the living room, but no sign of Judd. I walk out back and drool runs down my face.

Tight jeans. No shirt. His tan skin glistens, his muscles rippling as he works. I freeze in place, just gawking at him. I wipe my chin, the only movement my body is capable of at this moment.

Fuck, he's the hottest man I've ever seen. And he's all mine! I'm so lost in thought, I don't hear Lexi come up behind me.

"Hey girl, whatcha doing?"

Unable to speak, I just point.

"Oh, damn. Why are you standing here with me and not riding that?"

My cheeks heat, but that's nothing compared to the heat building down south. I nudge my friend's arm, and she laughs. Judd looks up, and a wide smile spreads across his face.

"He looks like he wants to devour you."

"Shut up!"

Lexi doubles over, as she snorts uncontrollably.

"You're such a dork," I tease.

"Like you aren't thinking about licking that chest."

"Oh my god, Lexi."

She ignores me and says, "Well, you could always, you know, help him shower. I'm sure he's tired after working all day."

"That sounds like a good idea," Judd says, stifling a laugh.

My cheeks turn an ever deeper shade of crimson.

"Well, what do ya say? Wanna wash me?" he asks with a teasing grin that just makes me wetter.

"See ya later, Lexi," I say. She laughs as she heads back home. I swear she comes over here just to tease me. But, whatever, I only have one thing on my dirty little mind right now.

We're sitting out in the garden watching Daisy and Lily play. As the sun sets, the sky lights up with the most beautiful colors. A content sigh escapes my lips as I lay my head on Judd's shoulder. He kisses the top of my head, and my insides melt.

I don't know what I'd do if I ever lost this amazing man.

Without warning, a feeling of dread washes through me, and I shiver.

"Are you cold?" Judd asks, concerned. I love that about him. He's so caring.

"The breeze is a little chilly," I fib.

He pulls me tight, and I feel a pang of guilt. I try to shake the feeling off, but it nags at me for the rest of the night.

I pull into the driveway after another trying day at work. Judd's working out in the backyard like he usually does. Damn, that man looks so good.

As I'm walking to the backyard, Judd moves further away from me. I stand and watch, gawking like I always do at those incredible muscles. He turns to look at me, then moves further away. He keeps going until I can no longer see him.

I try to scream, but my voice is gone. Tears spill over as my body trembles. Judd's gone.

I hear my sister's voice say, "And he's never coming back."

I collapse to my knees, the pain unbearable. All I can do is sob, so many tears that I'm drenched. I feel like I'm drowning. No matter how hard I try, I can't catch my breath.

"Mel? Mel!" I hear Judd's voice say. My body rocks as I hear his voice again, louder this time. "Mel!"

I spring up to a sitting position and realize I'm in bed. "What happened?" I ask.

Judd wraps his arms around me and hugs me tight. "You were having a nightmare. Do you remember anything?"

"Yeah." I fill Judd in on what happened.

"Baby, I'm not going anywhere," he says, pulling me closer and swaying gently with me. My heart pounds against my chest, and I'm drenched in sweat. Judd strokes my hair with his strong hand, and I feel calm washing over me.

Well, almost. I still can't shake that nagging feeling.

The next afternoon, I pull into the driveway and find out why. My tires screech as I race out of the driveway, tears pricking my eyes.

Chapter Four

Judd

I'm just getting ready to grab a shower before Mel gets home when I hear a car pull into my driveway.

She must have left work early.

I reach the driveway and see a cab. I'm about to ask the driver what address he's looking for when I see the passenger door open. My jaw drops when I see her.

What the fuck is she doing here?

I stand there, unable to make my feet move, as she approaches.

"Hey, stranger," she says.

That's it. After twenty years. After the way we left things, how can she be standing in my driveway?

Panic strikes me. Mel will be home any minute. And I've never told her about Abby. Fuck, why did I keep this from her? *Because you're a coward, asshole.*

I shake away the thoughts and narrow my eyes. "What are you doin' here?"

"I missed my cowboy."

"Bullshit. What the hell do you want?"

"Is that any way to treat your fiancée?"

"Ex-fiancée, remember?"

"That's water under the bridge. I miss you. You can't tell me you haven't missed me."

"Uh, yeah I can. You dumped me. I did the right thing, and you fuckin' turned on me. Now, again," I seethe through gritted teeth, "what are you doing here? How did you find out where I live?"

"You sold your father's ranch. You know that's public record."

"Yeah, that's public record. Not when I moved here or my address. My address here is not a matter of public record."

"You know damn well how small the community you betrayed is. It was easy to get the information."

"My fuckin' father kills my mother, but I'm the bad guy? Fuck that shit. And I still don't understand why you came here."

"It's been a long time. Can't we try again?" Her pout annoys me.

"Not long enough. I have a good life here, including a woman I love more than life itself. More than *anyone* I've loved before."

"Ouch." It's obvious how fake she's being.

"Yeah? Good. How do you think I felt when everyone turned on me? Now, get the fuck off my property."

She looks at me suspiciously. "You sure seem in a hurry to get rid of me."

"Because I don't want you here."

She crosses her arms over her chest. "Nah, it's more than that."

I just stare at her emotionless even though I'm pissed, and she's pushing me. "None of your damn business."

"There's someone else."

"I just said that. But again, none of your business."

"I bet she doesn't hold a candle to me."

I give her a cocky grin. "Darlin' you don't even come close."

"Oh, is that so? Well, does she kiss like this?"

Before I can react, Abby's arms are around my neck, and her lips are on mine. As I'm trying to push her away, I hear tires squeal. I get Abby away from me just in time to see Mel flying out of the driveway and speeding away. Anger courses through my veins as I shove her off me.

"Are you happy now? GET. THE. FUCK. OFF. MY. PROPERTY."

"But -"

She needs to leave before my heart explodes. "No. Not another word. You may have just cost me the only thing good that's ever happened to me. I never want to see your fucking face again."

I dial the local cab company and order a ride for Abby.

I need to find my woman. How the hell am I ever going to explain this? I try dialing her number, but it goes right to voicemail, so I try again. And again.

After the cab picks her up, I get in my truck and drive over to Damien's, but no sign of her car. Where else would she go? Jason's? Tammy's? Fuck, I can't lose her. I'm just past Damien's driveway when my cell rings, so I pull over.

"What the fuck did you do to my friend?" I hear Jason's voice yell into the phone.

"It wasn't my fault."

"Oh, it wasn't your mouth that woman was kissing. How could you do this to her?"

My ribs feel like they're squeezing me to death. "Please, I need to talk to her. I need to explain."

"She's sitting in my living room sobbing. Not sure that's a good idea."

"Please, man."

"Hold on."

Silence. Deafening silence while I wait. The feeling in the pit of my stomach is unbearable.

"She doesn't want to see you, man."

I close my eyes. "But if I could explain."

"No. Not tonight."

I hear footsteps and a door.

"Look, please just give her tonight. Call me tomorrow, and we'll see."

"But she's my girl." I don't know whether to cry or storm over there and haul her back with me.

"I know, but please, respect her wishes."

I take a breath to steady myself. "But she doesn't have a change of clothes or anything else she needs with her."

"I know. Tammy's on her way to your house."

I don't want to agree to this, but I know Mel needs time. "Fine, but only because I love Mel. I'll have a bag ready."

"Thanks, man. Level with me, though. Promise me there's nothing going on with this other woman."

"I promise. I just need to be able to tell Mel first."

"I understand."

Jay hangs up without saying another word, so I turn around and head back home. I'm just coming downstairs with a bag when I hear the doorbell. Tammy's stands on the other side, a look of concern on her face. Not sure what to say, I shove the bag at her.

"Just give her time. Jay and I are going to talk to her and try to get her to talk to you."

"Thank you," I sigh.

"You got it." I watch Tammy walk to her car and head out. Daisy and Lily sit on either side of me. I give them each a pat on the head then slink over to the couch and throw myself down. The dogs follow me and settle with me, a furry head on each leg.

I've never been more thankful to have them than I am right now. But, damn it, this house is empty without my woman. I just hope seeing Abby didn't fuck things up beyond repair. I pray she's on a plane as we speak.

I hear the doorbell followed by a chorus of barks. I must have forgotten something in the bag I packed. I shuffle over to the door.

"Dude, you look like hell," Damien says when I open the door.

"Nothin' compared to how I feel."

"What's goin' on?"

"I don't even know where to start."

I grab two beers and motion Damien to the living room. He sits in the recliner, and I park my loser ass back on the couch.

"Talk to me, man. I heard Mel peel outta here earlier."

"She got home from work and saw another woman kissing me."

"I beg your pardon?" Damien's eyes widen, and his mouth hangs open.

"Look, there's somethin' I haven't told anyone about my time in Texas. I was engaged."

"What?!" His eyebrows shoot up.

"Yeah. The daughter of one of my dad's rancher buddies. When everything went down, she dumped me."

"Then how did Mel see her kissing you?"

"Outta the fuckin' blue, she shows up today."

"Damn, man."

"I just got done telling her about Mel when she grabbed me and kissed. I was pushing her away just as Mel was flying back out of the driveway."

"But you explained what happened, right?"

"I didn't get a chance. She's staying at Jay's tonight, and she didn't wanna talk to me. Tammy came and picked up some stuff."

"I don't know what to say, man. I'm sorry. But listen, you two love each other. You'll get through this."

"Oh? How can you be so damn sure? How would Lexi feel?" I pause before shaking my head. "Sorry, man, that was outta line."

"No worries. I know the pain you're in. Lexi and I hit a couple of rough patches at the beginning."

I sigh, my heart aching at the thought of Mel not being in my arms tonight. No one knows how I feel better than Damien.

"We have a guest room. And the dogs love each other."

"Thanks, man, but won't Lexi be pissed about what I did?"

"Dude, first off, you didn't do anything. And Lexi will understand. She may even have some advice."

"Alright. Let me just get some stuff together for me and the dogs."

"Okay."

Damien helps me load the dogs into my truck, then we drive to his house. Lexi's waiting in the kitchen when we get inside. She grabs a beer for Damien and me, then pours herself a glass of wine.

"Tell me what happened," she says, her hand lightly on my arm.

I fill her in on the whole sordid story as tears threaten to spill. "I don't know what I'm gonna do if she won't listen to me."

"She will. She just needs time. Imagine the shock she felt when she saw someone kissing you."

"If only she had stayed a little longer, she woulda seen me push Abby away"

"I know, but you need to look at it from her perspective. You know how insecure she was before you two got together. I'm sure that all came rushing back to her. I'm not blaming you, please know that, but maybe if you'd told her about Abby, she would have reacted different."

"You're right, and believe me, I'm kicking myself right now. That's why I need her to let me explain."

"What did Jay say?" Lexi asks.

"He said to give her time, and to try calling tomorrow."

"Then, and I know this is hard, but that's what you need to do. I'll call her tomorrow and see if I can convince her."

"Thanks, Lexi, but I don't wanna push her too hard."

"I know. I got it covered. You two are made for each other. We're going to fight for her."

I give her a weak smile. "I can't thank you both enough. I hope this doesn't sound rude, but I'm exhausted."

"Not rude at all. You go get some rest. Damien and I will take care of the dogs."

I nod and slowly walk to the guest room. Just the thought of sleeping without Mel kills me. The way she cuddles against me, her sweet little snores, the intoxicating scent of her shampoo. Just her.

I get ready for bed but sleep is nowhere to be found. All I can think about is her sobbing, her heart broken at what she saw. Fuck, I screwed up.

Chapter Five

Judd

The next morning, the scent of bacon and fresh-brewed coffee fills my nose. I walk out just as Lexi's finishing up cooking. She gives Damien and I each a plate of food then fixes one for herself. Damien serves the coffee. Not wanting to seem rude, I force myself to eat, even though that's the last thing I want.

The only thing I want is my woman. I'm tempted to call. Jay said I could call today, after all, but I'm sure Mel is on her way to work, and I don't want her going there upset. She has enough trouble with Daniel. I don't wanna make things worse.

"Any plans today?" Damien asks.

"Just my usual. Hoping work will keep my mind off things. Or, at least, ease it a little bit."

"You're welcome to leave the dog here for the day. We were planning to take our goofballs to the dog park in a bit," Lexi says.

"Are you sure? Four is a lot."

"Yeah, but Mel did an amazing job training them." She bites her lip when she realizes she said Mel's name. "Sorry."

"No, it's okay. She did. If you're sure, that would be great."

"You got it, man," Damien says.

After I help Damien clean up, I head back to the farm and get to work. Hard as I try, of course, I can't stop thinking about Mel. After I shower, I drive over and pick up two very sleepy dogs. Once we're home, I call Jay's cell.

"I tried man, but she's not ready."

"But I really need to talk to her."

"I know, and I'm sorry. I promise I'll keep trying. For now, just give her the space she needs."

"I can't. Please, Jay, I can't live without her. I'm trying to respect the space, but this could all be resolved if I could just talk to her."

"I know, man, really I do, but pushing her now might push her away for good."

I disconnect and slam the phone down with an angry huff. How the fuck can he keep me from my girl? I know if I could just get a few minutes with her, she'd understand.

I feel like I'm going to explode, so I take the dogs out back for some exercise. I see Damien and Lexi outside, so I walk over to the fence.

"I'm guessing by the look on your face you didn't get to talk to Mel," Lexi says.

"Jay said she's not ready. I'm just not sure how much longer I can wait."

"I'll be back," Lexi says as she walks toward her house.

"Man, I wish there was more I could do," Damien says.

"Keep me from kicking Jay's ass. He's keeping my woman from me."

"I get how you feel, man, but you know that won't make things better."

"I know. I'm just pissed that any of this happened. Most of all, though, I hate the thought of Mel hurting."

"Yeah, it sucks."

"Hey, guys, I talked to Mel," Lexi says when she joins us.

"And?" I say, nerves sending my stomach flipping.

"She agreed to have lunch with me tomorrow, so I'm taking food to her office. I'll keep trying."

It's a small glimmer of hope, but I'll take it. "I can't thank you enough."

"We're gonna fix this. I promise," Lexi says, tears in her eyes. "Until then, would you care to join us for dinner? You could bring the dogs over, and I'll get some burgers ready."

"Sure, thanks." It's better than being alone.

I hand the dogs over the fence one at a time to Damien, and they take off to play with Dave and Maggie. I climb over the fence and walk with Damien to the grill while Lexi goes inside. She returns a few minutes later with a plate of burgers.

"I'll cook since you were kind enough to invite me," I say.

"Thanks, man. I'm gonna go help Lexi inside."

I stand at the grill alone cooking the burgers. Well, not alone. Four dogs are sitting around me, drool dripping from their furry little faces. I can't help but smile a little seeing them.

When the burgers are done, I put them on the clean plate Lexi left with me and carry them to the table, four dogs hot on my heels praying for one of those burgers to hit the ground.

Lexi and Damien come out with a salad, rolls, and beer. We all make up plates and sit down to eat. The dogs finally give up and head down to play while we finish up.

I'm helping clean up when I hear a car pull into my driveway. I walk over to the fence, and my blood boils when I see who's standing there.

"What the fuck are you still doing here?" I shout when I see Abby getting out of a car.

"I couldn't go home the way we left things."

"Do you have any idea what you've cost me? I don't want you here!"

I hear the grass rustle behind me. "Bitch, I'd highly recommend getting the fuck out of here," Lexi says.

"And just who the hell are you? The girlfriend?" Abby asks.

"No, I'm the girlfriend's best friend. And I'm beyond furious that you've hurt two of the most special people in my life."

"Mind your own business, bitch," Abby spits.

Before anyone can react, I see Lexi's arm whiz past my head. Her fist connects with Abby's face, knocking her on her ass. I stand there, mouth hanging open. I look at Damien, and he's also standing there, jaw open wide.

"What the hell is your problem?" Abby screams.

"First is what you did to Judd all those years ago, then what you did when you came here, and finally, for calling me a bitch. Now, do us all a favor and get the fuck out of here."

Abby screams in frustration and stomps off rubbing her jaw. She gets in her car and flies out of my driveway as she takes off. I can only hope it's to the airport.

"I'm sorry," Lexi says.

"Don't be. She had it coming," Judd says.

"Yeah, but what if I caused you more trouble?"

"Then, I'll deal with it. Really, Lexi, don't worry." I side hug her.

"Okay. Just thinking about what she did to my best friend." She leans into me. "Listen, just hang in there. I'll let you know where things stand after we have lunch tomorrow."

"Thank you again, Lexi. For dinner, for your support, everything. You too, Damien. I'm exhausted, so I'm gonna call it a night."

"I'll go round up the dogs," Lexi says.

"Go take care of your wife's hand," I say to Damien with a proud grin.

"You got it. Like she said, keep hanging in there."

"I will."

I take the girls inside and get ready for bed, but like the night before, sleep is nowhere to be found. I grab my phone and scroll through some photos of Mel. Damn, I need her here. I miss her warm body next to me in bed.

The next day drags. All I can think about is Lexi having lunch with Mel, and hoping Mel will agree to listen to me. I got a text from Damien letting me know she still wasn't ready, so all I can do is wait.

Two weeks go by, and I feel like I'm losing my mind. I've lost count of the number of times I drove to Jay's house, determined to make her listen. But every time, I came to my senses and gave her the space she asked for.

Another Friday arrives, which means another lonely weekend. I'm just walking into the kitchen after my shower when the doorbell rings. Figuring Lexi's here to tell me the bad news in person, I nearly pull the door off the hinges. My anger dissipates when I see who's standing on the other side.

Chapter Six

Judd

"I'm ready to talk," Mel whispers, her voice raspy. I gaze at her face, and my heart shatters. Her bloodshot eyes and tear-stained cheeks feel like a punch in the gut.

"Please, come in, and have a seat." I try to take her hand, but she pulls it away.

She sits down on the couch and gets attacked by two wiggly butts. A brief smile lights up her beautiful face, but it disappears when I sit in the chair next to the couch.

"Let me know when you're ready," I say.

"As ready as I'll ever be to get dumped."

"Why would you think that?" It's a question I shouldn't have asked. I know what she saw.

"Oh please. I saw you kissing that woman." She doesn't look at me.

"I know what it looked like, but I promise you, she kissed me."

"Yeah, right. It was only a matter of time before you realized there was someone better out there." I hate how defeated she sounds.

"Look, there's something I never told you about my father's arrest."

She looks at me, finally, but doesn't say anything, so I continue.

"I was engaged at the time. The daughter of one of my dad's friends. When the news broke that I was the one who turned my father in, she threw the ring at me and broke things off. It was then that I realized she wasn't the one. If she was, she wouldn't have turned on me."

She nibbles her lip. "Sorry."

"Then, out of the blue, she shows up here, telling me she misses me. I was trying to get her to leave. I told her I had someone.. When I told her that she didn't even come close to being as good as you, she grabbed me and kissed me. I was trying to push her away when I heard you drive away. I'm so sorry. I never wanted to hurt you."

Mel lets out a huge breath. "I know, and I appreciate you explaining." She looks down at her hands, and I can tell she's ashamed of her reaction. I don't like that she'd feel like she needs to feel shame in the first place. "I hope you understand why I reacted the way I did."

"Of course, baby. I wanted so bad to knock Jay's door down and make you listen."

"That sounds like something out of a movie." A small laugh escapes her, a sound that makes my heart flutter.

"Please, tell me how we fix this."

"I wanna come home."

"Are you sure? I don't want to push you."

"You're not. I can't stand the thought of another night without you." She sniffles before looking at me hopefully. "Is she gone?"

"I hope so. Lexi decked her."

Her smile grows. "She told me. I kinda wish I could have seen it."

"It was badass!" I can't help the pride that crosses my face.

"Do you mind if I call Jay quick and let him know I'm staying?"

"You don't need my permission."

"You're sweet."

After she disconnects, we take the dogs out back. We head to the garden to watch them play.

"I missed this. Missed those girls. But most of all, I missed you."

"I missed you, too, my sweet angel. I love you so much."

"I love you, too." She turns her head toward mine and leans in. I grab her head and pull her into me, kissing her harder than ever before.

Her tongue dances with mine as we get lost in each other, trying to make up for lost time.

Loud barking interrupts our make out session. I look up and see both girls at the fence. Damien and Lexi stand on the other side, dopey grins on their faces, while the four furries greet each other.

"May we help you?" I ask.

"We're so happy," Lexi says, her eyes glistening. Mel runs over and hugs her friend across the fence. The ladies whisper to each other while Damien and I watch.

"We need to celebrate, man," Damien says.

"How about dinner at our house tomorrow night?" Mel asks.

"It's the least we can do after the support you gave us," I add.

"And of course, you better bring Dave and Maggie, too," Mel says.

"You know, Dave has it made. Three pretty ladies love him!" Damien jokes, and we all laugh. But of course, no laugh makes me happier than the one coming from my woman.

"Do you need us to keep the dogs at our house so they don't see anything, um, naughty?" Lexi teases.

"Oh, trust me, they've already seen plenty," Mel says.

Damien pats me on the shoulder. "Way to go, man."

"Seriously, though, I'm so glad everything worked out," Lexi says. Turning to her husband, she adds, "Let's leave the lovebirds alone."

After she and Damien head home, we let Daisy and Lily play until the sun sets, then head inside.

"Be right back. Have a seat on the couch," Mel says with a wink.

And there goes my dick.

She walks back out, and I almost pass out cold. She stands before me in a black silk nightgown that stops mid-thigh. The lacy top features a beautiful flower pattern sheer enough to give me a peek at her sexy cleavage. Her long blonde hair hangs loose around her shoulders, and her lips are painted bright red, matching her nails.

Damn, there's no more beautiful woman on this planet. She saunters over to me and straddles my lap. Running my hands under the nightie, I discover she's going commando, and damn again, I love how her soft skin feels in my hands.

"Baby, I want you so much," I say huskily.

"Oh, Judd, I want you more." She lifts her nightie over her head and tosses it aside while my eyes soak in her incredible body.

Her hands make their way under my shirt before she removes it and presses her incredible chest against mine. She crushes her lips to mine, her tongue aggressively exploring my mouth. She stops and stands, gazing at me.

"Up and out of those pants. Now!"

Damn, I love when she takes charge like this. I get naked at record speed.

"That's a good cowboy. Now, get that naked ass back on the couch."

I sit and just stare at her, my dick aching for her. She slips her fingers between her legs, teasing her sweet pussy while I watch.

"Is that turning you on, sexy?"

"Mmm, yeah, baby."

"Show me how much. I wanna see you strokin' that huge cock."

She licks her lips as I start pumping my dick, and fuck, all I can think about is that mouth wrapped around me.

As if she can read my mind, she gets on her knees in front of me, grabs my hand, and moves it off my dick. When I feel those soft, pouty lips wrap around my erection, I nearly explode. Her head bobs up and down, her hair tickling my legs while long red nails rake my chest.

"So good, woman. Mmm, baby, I wanna taste you."

She moans, and the vibrations feel incredible. My balls tighten as she pushes me over the edge, and I fill her pretty little mouth. Locking eyes with me, she swallows and licks her lips after she pops her mouth off me before she gets up and sits on the couch, spreading those creamy thighs wide.

The scent of her desire fills the air, and it's intoxicating. I kneel before my queen and slide my tongue between her folds, forcing a moan from her throat.

"Judd," she moans as I give her a couple more swipes with my tongue. My lips find her clit, and I suck hard while I slide my fingers inside her soaking wet pussy. "You taste so damn good."

"Please don't stop."

I continue my assault until I feel her body tremble. She screams as she writhes beneath me, soaking my fingers. I pull them out and lap up her tangy juices.

"Ass back on that couch, cowboy."

I scramble to my feet and do as I'm told. She climbs onto my lap, taking my entire length inside her pussy. I slide in easily after her orgasm. She slowly moves up and down my dick, driving me wild. I try to increase the pace, and she stops.

"No, no, no, my naughty cowboy." She just sits there on my dick. "Behave yourself, or you're in trouble."

"Oh, is that so?" I drawl with a teasing smirk.

"Keep it up, and I'm gonna give you a good spanking."

"Do you promise?" I smile and bounce beneath her.

"Oh, so you like that, huh?"

"Yeah."

"Yes, ma'am," she corrects me. "On your feet." She climbs off of me, and I stand. "Good cowboy. Now, bend over the couch."

I bend at the waist, using my hands to brace myself and wiggle my ass at her. I groan when I feel her soft little hand swat my ass. After several more swats, each harder than the one before it, my dick is aching to be back inside her.

"Are you ready to be a good cowboy?"

"Yes, ma'am."

"Good answer. Now fuck me in a way you've never done before. And I better like it."

I smirk. "Sit tight, love." I head for the bedroom. When I return to the living room, a smile spreads across Mel's face as she stares at me in my black, leather, ass-less chaps and matching cowboy hat.

"Oh my god, babe! I need to ride you now!"

As soon as I sit down, she climbs back onto my lap, and I'm back inside of her. This time, though, she rides me hard and fast.

I can't take my eyes off her sexy breasts bouncing in front of me. I pull her in tight against my chest, drinking in her delicious scent as we fuck. I unload inside her as her body trembles with her own orgasm. Her body goes limp against mine, and she sighs as I hold her close.

I press my lips against her neck. "I love you, my sweet angel."

"I love you, my cowboy."

Chapter Seven

Mel

"Good morning, sunshine," Jay says on his way past my office.

"Morning."

"You okay?"

"Fine."

"Mel. I know you better than that. Did something happen with Judd?"

"Nah, we're fine."

He watches me for a moment. "I'm not leaving here until you tell me."

Arms crossed, Jay comes in and sits down. *Stubborn ass.*

"I just have this nagging fear we haven't heard the last of Abby."

"I thought she went back to Texas."

"Judd assumed she did after Lexi punched her, but I'm not convinced."

"You can't think like that."

"Trust me, my rational side knows that. But my emotional side is kicking that side's ass right now."

"I'd tell you not to dwell on it, but I know you better."

"I'm really trying not to. Maybe the nagging feeling is something else. I don't know."

"Or it could be nothing."

"True, but it's been all quiet from my sister, too, which worries me. Then, there's wondering when Daniel's going to get his wish."

"Have you given any more thought to quitting?" Jay says after a few moments.

"I have, but I'm not ready to give in just yet. Plus, what if I lose Judd?"

"Are you trying to make me kick your cute butt? You're not gonna lose him. That dude is crazy about you."

"He told you he doesn't like Abby, didn't he?" I ask worriedly.

"Yeah."

"And has he lied to you before?"

"No. So, why would he lie now?"

"I don't know."

"Listen, tough love time. You're making more out of this than it is. And I'm only saying this 'cause I hate what it's doing to you. I want my friend back."

"I'm still here."

"Yeah, but you're not yourself."

"I'm trying."

"I know you are. I'm always available if you need to talk. Tammy is, too."

"Thanks."

After a few moments, Jay says, "Hey, maybe a night out is what you need. Tammy's off on Saturday night, so how about karaoke?"

"I'll check with Judd. Damien and Lexi are coming for dinner tonight, so I'll text you after."

"Cool. I better run before King Dickhead shows up."

I force a smile and wave as Jay heads off to his office.

When I get home, I grab a quick shower and change, then help Judd get dinner ready. We're just finishing up when our two-legged and four-legged guests appear at the back door. I motion them to come in.

The second Damien opens the sliding glass door, Daisy and Lily take off, nearly knocking him over, and four furry flashes fly around the back yard.

"I thought I was a goner," Damien jokes.

"All your fault. Dave's a stud," I tease.

"Need any help?" Lexi asks.

"Everything's ready, so just carrying stuff outside," I say.

"Put me to work while the men go play with fire."

Judd takes the Filet Mignon out to the grill and starts cooking while Lexi and I carry everything else outside. As soon as Judd brings the platter over to the table, four furry-butts beeline towards the food,, forming a circle around us.

"I think they're plotting something," Judd jokes.

"If they are, Dave's the mastermind," Damien says.

"Yeah, and those girls will do anything the stud tells them to," Lexi teases.

For the first time in too long, I feel relaxed, and I laugh at the thought of the four of them plotting to steal our dinner.

That feeling is short-lived when I hear a familiar voice.

"Where's my damn sister?"

Ugh. Trish. Lexi sits up straight, balling her fists.

"Calm down, Lexi Balboa," Damien warns.

"What are you doing here?" I ask.

"I need to get my car fixed."

"Then go to a garage."

"How am I supposed to pay for it?"

"Well, most people use money," I say calmly.

"Oh ha, ha, bitch. You know I don't have any."

"Yep. And?"

"Do I have to spell it out for you?"

"No. I know exactly why you're here and what you want. But nothing's changed. I'm not a damn bank."

"Then what am I supposed to do?"

I shrug. "Get a job."

"I have one, idiot."

"Then get a second one."

"Why should I do that when you have money?"

"Are you fucking serious?" My resolve is about to snap.

"I'm family. You have to help me."

"The hell I do. You're an adult and perfectly capable of earning your own money. The only ones I'm obligated to are those two dogs out there."

"Oh, so you'll spend money on them but not on me?"

"Ding, ding, ding, tell her what she's won. Oh, hey, there's an idea. Fly to California and go on The Price is Right."

I hear Lexi snort behind me, followed by deep laughs from Damien and Judd.

"You're all so fuckin' funny," Trish huffs.

"We try."

"You know, if you keep treating me like this, I'm gonna stop talking to you," Trish threatens.

"You promise?" I ask sarcastically as I flutter my eyelashes at her.

Trish's face turns bright red, as she grunts and gives me the finger before she turns and storms out of our backyard. Judd, Damien, and Lexi are still laughing. I join them, at least on the outside. My insides, however, are churning.

Why can't I seem to catch a break? If it isn't Daniel or Judd's newly-revealed ex-fiancée, then it's my sister trying to send me over the edge.

I let my go-to calming song, *Avalon* by Sully Erna, run through my head, easing my tension slightly. I grab my glass of wine and chug it.

"You okay?" Judd asks.

"Fine."

Everyone stares at me, waiting for me to say something else.

"What?" I snap.

"After what happened and the way you just downed that glass, are you sure?" Lexi asks.

I can see everyone's concern. "I just said I was fine."

Nobody says a word. They just sit and stare. Suddenly feeling restless, I jump up and start clearing the table. As I'm standing alone in the kitchen, I can see the three of them talking. It brings tears to my eyes.

Oh, that's really nice. Just sit and talk about me. The loser with all the baggage. Judd's gonna dump me for sure.

My insides feel like they're being pulled apart as my insecurities take over. I see Lexi heading inside with some of the dishes, so I plaster a smile on face.

"We didn't mean to upset you," Lexi says.

"You didn't. I just know Judd's gonna send me packing."

She looks at me in shock. "Why would you think that?"

"Too much baggage."

She shakes her head. "Stop it, girl. Every time that guy looks at you, he looks like a hungry lion. He loves you!"

"For now."

I walk outside to grab more stuff before Lexi can say anything else. I'll just sit here and wait for my life to implode. I know it's coming. I just hope I'm ready. The only question is what I'll lose first. My cowboy? My dogs? My job? My friends? Everything?

After Lexi and Damien are gone, Judd and I sit down by the garden. I glance over at him. His chiseled features, sexy muscles, the way he works a pair of jeans like no other man. The thought of losing him burns a hole in my stomach, and I shudder.

Judd puts his arms around me and pulls me in close. "Are you sure you're okay?" Judd asks.

"Yeah, why?"

"Well, you seemed a little short earlier."

I huff. "I was not. Why's everyone always on my damn case?"

"Hey. I'm not trying to get on your case. I love you, and I'm worried about you."

I shrug. "Stop worrying. I'm fine."

Except that I couldn't be further from fine, but I can't tell him that.

Just the idea of him finding out what a mess I am on the inside will cost me everything. The time I spent at Jay's, away from my cowboy's arms, were torture, and I don't want to go through that again. As long as I can keep convincing him that everything is good, he'll keep me.

Chapter Eight

Mel

The following Friday morning, I'm sitting in my office working and minding my own business when Daniel appears in my doorway.

But he's not alone, and when I see her, my blood runs cold. The smirk on Daniel's face tells me he knows exactly who this is.

"Good morning, Melissa. I'd like to introduce you to my new executive assistant, Abigail Donaldson. Going forward, she'll be in charge of handling the other executives. I trust that won't be an issue for you."

"Not at all, Daniel. Welcome, Abigail," I say with a fake smile I hope looks convincing.

Abby tosses her hair and glares at me. "Thank you."

"Staff meeting in one hour," Daniel says before he and Abby leave my office.

I fall into my chair, unable to catch my breath. Why is she here? Why didn't she go back to Texas? How am I going to handle being in the same room with her, being civil to her? I feel like an elephant is sitting on my chest.

A few minutes pass, and Jay pops in. "Mel, what's wrong?" I don't know how, but he always just knows. "Did Daniel stop by your office?"

"Yeah, with his new assistant."

I bury my head in my hands.

"I don't understand. Why is this an issue?"

Lifting my head, tears in my eyes, I just stare at Jay. All of a sudden, his eyes go wide and his jaw drops, just like Joey does on *Friends*.

"She's *that* Abby."

My forehead slams into the desk as I start to shake, gulping as I sob. "I'm gonna lose Judd," I choke.

"You are not."

"Yeah, right. He's gonna remember why he loved her, and that'll be it for me. I can't compare to her."

"You're right, you can't. You're a million light years better than her."

Yeah, right. She's gorgeous. Plain old boring me will never live up to her. And now, I have to deal with her every day. How the hell am I gonna get through this damn meeting?

Without warning, my stomach churns, and I run off to my private restroom. Sinking to the floor, I hang my head over the toilet.

I hear a light knock at the door. "You okay, Mel?"

"I'll be right out." *No, I'm not okay. I couldn't be further from okay.* I moisten a paper towel and bury my face in it. I look in the mirror, and I'm horrified at the image looking back at me. "Can you do me a favor?" I call out to Jay.

"Anything."

"Can you see if Allie can come down?"

"On it."

A few minutes later, I hear another knock. "Mel, it's me," Allie says.

"I need your help. Please."

Allie comes in and says, "What can I do?"

"Can you help me fix my makeup? I can't go to the meeting looking like this."

She grabs a chair from my office and pushes it into the restroom. "Sit." Allie grabs my makeup bag off the counter and gets to work. She holds up a small mirror in front of me when she's done. "How's that?" she asks.

"Thank you so much," I say with relief. I look much more me.

"I feel like we're Claire and Allison at the end of *The Breakfast Club*," Allie teases when we come out of the bathroom.

"And who does that make me?" Jay asks.

Allie and I look at each and, in unison, we both say, "Brian."

"Hey! He was the geek."

"If the pocket protector fits," I tease.

"Ah, there's my girl." Allie smiles.

"Yeah, we'll see what's left of her after the meeting," Jay responds.

"The staff meeting?" Allie asks. "Daniel giving you trouble again?"

"If only," I say. Allie's been so busy with new hires that I hadn't had a chance to fill her in. So, Jay and I tell her the whole sordid tale.

"Oh, sweetie, I'm so sorry. But everything's okay now?"

"For now, but what happens when Judd finds out she's still here?"

"Nothing," Allie says. "He adores you, and nothing's gonna change that."

How can everybody be so certain of that? Well, they're all wrong. I know better. I'm gonna end up all alone, and hey, that's probably what I deserve anyway. After all, I'm damaged goods. No, stop, not now, I chide myself.

Allie just spent all that time fixing my makeup. I can't start crying again. Besides, it's almost time to head to the boardroom. Grabbing my favorite notebook and pen, I say, "Let's go get this over with."

Somehow, I manage to survive the meeting, but I can't wait to get out of there. Normally, I can't wait to go home, but even that doesn't make me feel better. Judd's going to ask me about my day, filling me with dread. I can't tell him about Abby, but not telling him is the same as lying. What the hell am I gonna do?

I take a different way home, and stop by the park. I walk to the dock and take a seat on the bench, just gazing out at the sun dancing on the water, losing all track of time. The sounds of my cell ringing snaps me out of my reverie. I see Judd's name on the screen, but I let it go to voicemail.

After a few minutes, I play his message. "Baby, it's me. Where are you? Dinner's been ready, and I haven't heard from you. Call me when you get this. Love you."

I put my phone away without calling back, staying at the park until dusk. Knowing the park closes at sundown, I finally head home. When I pull into the driveway, I see Damien, Lexi, Jay, and Tammy sitting there with Judd, who flies off the porch when he sees me.

"Where were you?" Judd exclaims.

"What do you mean?" I ask, bewildered.

"It's late, and I had no idea where you were."

"And?" I blink.

"And I was worried. What's going on?"

"Nothing. Why? And what the hell is everyone doing here?"

"We were all worried. Nobody knew where you were."

"Yeah, well I'm here now, and I'm fine, so they can go home."

"Mel," Judd begins.

"No, I just wanna be alone."

I stand by my car, refusing to move. Maybe I'm being bratty, but I don't care. This is all going to end soon anyway. Better if it's on my terms. Judd sighs and walks back to the porch. Once everyone's gone, I walk inside.

"Hungry? I can heat some food up for you."

"Nah, just wanna go to sleep."

"Please, babe, come talk to me first. Did something happen today?"

"No, I'm fine."

"Come on, you haven't been yourself. I know something's botherin' you."

"I'm fine. I swear."

"I guess, but I'm not convinced. Now, please at least come eat a little something."

"I'm fine, I just wanna go to bed."

I head off to the bathroom to wash my face and get ready for bed. When I hear Judd come out of the bathroom, I roll onto my side, away from his side of the bed, and pretend I'm asleep. When I'm sure Judd's asleep, I sneak out of bed and pad to the kitchen to grab a snack. I curl up on the couch and turn the TV on.

The next morning, I awaken to the hot breath of two furry faces panting in my face. Judd sits in the recliner staring at me, his brow furrowed.

"Couldn't sleep, sweetie?" he asks.

"No, and I didn't want to wake you, so I came out here."

He's quiet for a long time. "Are you sure nothing's wrong? Here or at work?"

"I'm sure. Like I told you, I'm fine."

"You keep saying that, but -"

"I promise, you'll be the first to know."

He still doesn't look convinced. "I'll accept that for now, but we're not done talking. Now, what can I fix you for breakfast?"

"I'm good, I'll get something at work."

"You promise? You need to eat."

"I will." After a quick shower, I get dressed. Before I leave, I pat the dogs on the head, grab my stuff, give Judd a quick kiss and head off to another day of dodging not one, but two enemies.

Chapter Nine

Judd

After Mel's gone, I give the girls their breakfast and take them out to the barn with me. All I can think about is the kiss I got from Mel. No passion, no desire, just a quick peck on the cheek. I know for sure something happened at work, but she won't tell me. When I asked Jay, I could tell by the look on his face that he knew, but he wouldn't tell me either.

I take the dogs and head out to the backyard, where I see Damien and Lexi sitting on their patio. They walk over to the fence, so I join them.

"Anything?" Lexi asks.

"She just keeps sayin' she's fine," I say. "But I know damn well she's not."

Lexi nods. "I can try. Do you think it's something at work?"

"Yeah. Jay's face gave it away. But for some reason, nobody wants to tell me."

"Let me see if I can get her to agree to dinner. No group outing, just me and her. I think she'll be more willing to talk without the other girls there."

"I agree, and I really can't thank you enough. Both of you." I sigh, missing my angel. The fun-loving angel she was when we first met.

Lexi and Damien stare at me, and the pity on their faces is making me crazy. The last thing I want is anyone feeling sorry for me.

Besides, the focus should be on Mel and figuring out what's going on. I watch Lexi take her phone out of the back pocket of her denim shorts. She puts the phone on speaker.

"Hey Lexi, what's up?" Just the sound of my girl's voice drives me wild.

"Any plans tonight?"

"Nothing special."

Ouch. A night home with me should be special.

"How about a good old-fashioned Melexi Pizza Party?"

"Wow, I haven't heard that in years."

"Too many years. So, whatta ya say?"

"Count me in. I just gotta change after work."

"Okay, I'll pick you up. Six work for you?"

"Yeah, thanks. And, Lexi, I'm really looking forward to it."

"Me too."

Lexi disconnects and turns to me, a smile on her face.

"Thank you," I say. I'm a little hurt, but a lot relieved that Lexi might get something out of her.

"You got it," Lexi says.

"Now, what the hell is Melexi?" Damien asks.

"Mel and Lexi, doofus," Lexi teases. "Back when we were silly singles, Friday nights were always our unwind and get crazy nights, and there was never a shortage of adult beverages. So one night, tipsy from wine, we coined the term as a way of mocking all those celebrity couples."

Damien and I laugh out loud, helping to relieve a little bit of my stress. I hope Lexi can get through to Mel tonight, at least get her talking. After thanking them again, I get back to work.

I make sure I'm waiting for her on the front porch when she gets home. My heart skips when I see her pull into the driveway. I'm so in love with this amazing woman, and it's killing me seeing her so down.

I hear Godsmack's music blasting as she pulls into the driveway. Shit. Daniel must have been giving her a hard time.

Meeting her at the car, I open her door and help her out. That earns me a small smile, and given how she's been feeling, I'll take it.

"Did you work later today?" she asks.

"No, why?"

"Usually you're cleaned up before I get home."

"Well, my arms were a bit tired today, so I thought you could help me."

"Oh, is that so? You think I want to get naked in a hot, steamy shower with you?"

"I hope so." I smile, but she has no idea how badly I want her to say yes. I just want her happy.

She walks toward the house, leaving me standing next to her car. Turning to me, she says, "Well, what the hell are you waiting for, cowboy?"

Mel

"You ready? Lexi's here," Judd yells.

"Just finishing up."

I come out just as Lexi's coming inside. Her jaw drops when she sees me. "Oh my god, you still have it?"

"Of course. It's my favorite!"

We had a friend who owned a t-shirt printing place back in our roommate days. He made us each a shirt that said Melexi in the center of a pizza. Lexi's eyes fill up with nostalgic tears as she looks at me.

"Mine's packed away, but you can bet I'll be digging it out."

I smile at my friend. As I pass Judd on my way to the door, I give him a smack on the ass. "Thanks for the shower." He always knows just what I need.

I know this feeling won't last, but for now, I'm relaxed and ready to enjoy dinner with my best friend. We hit a bit of a rocky patch, but we worked through it, and our friendship is stronger than ever.

"Have fun, ladies."

"We will," Lexi says. "Oh, Damien said to tell you that you're welcome to head over if you get bored."

"Thanks."

When we get inside Palermo's, Georgio, the owner, takes us to our favorite table.

"Can I get you ladies something to drink?"

"One bottle of Moscato and two glasses please," Lexi says.

After Giorgio goes to get our wine, Lexi asks, "What do you want to eat?"

"Gooey extra cheese and tons of pepperoni."

"Perfect." I tell Giorgio our order when he drops off the wine. "So, what made you wanna go out?"

"I wanted some girl time with my bestie. And, I wanna talk."

"What about?"

"You. Sweetie, you haven't been yourself lately. I'm worried about you."

"Just like I told Judd, I'm fine."

"You can't get away with that with me. I know you too well, my dear."

I grab my glass and chug my wine, then pour myself another.

"I know everything's okay with the sexy cowboy, so is it something at work?"

"Why do I have to keep telling everyone I'm fine?" I ask irritated.

"Because we know better. Please, you know it's better to talk about it."

"But there's nothin' to talk about." I down my second glass of wine and fill up again. Lexi catches up and before our pizza even comes, we've polished off the whole bottle.

Lexi orders a second one. They wait until the pizza's ready to bring it. I pour two more glasses while Lexi serves us each a slice of pizza.

"Now, I'm asking again. Please, Mel, talk to me."

"Well, there might be something, but Judd can't find out."

"It's not another man, is it?"

"Hell no." I pause for dramatic effect. "It's another woman."

"What?" Lexi nearly chokes on her wine, and I snort.

"Abby."

"His ex Abby?" Lexi's eyes go wide.

"Yeah. She's still here. And now, she's Daniel's assistant."

Lexi's mouth drops before she utters, "What in the ever-lovin' fuck? You have to tell Judd."

I shake my head back and forth. "I can't."

Lexi tilts her head to the side and says, "He deserves to know."

I shrug my shoulders. "Yeah, but what if he realizes he still loves her?"

Lexi holds her hand up. "Stop! You know there's no way in hell he loves her. He loves you more than anything."

I lower my head and sigh. "For now."

Lexi shakes her head at me, but doesn't say anything. We polish off the pizza as well as two more bottles of wine. We're both laughing so hard, we can barely breathe, but I have no idea what we're laughing about. I hear the bell that rings when the restaurant door opens.

"Oh, damn, look at those hot men," I yell.

"Yeah, and they're headed our way. Quick, get your boobs set," Lexi shouts.

Chapter Ten

Judd

A little while after the ladies head to dinner, I take Daisy and Lily next door. Damien grabs a couple of beers, and we sit out back while the dogs play.

"Hope Lexi can get through to Mel," Damien says.

"I'll drink to that." We clink bottles and each take a sip.

"Forgive me for asking, but is everything cool with you two?"

"Far as I know. Guessin' it's either Trish or Daniel causing her mood."

"Makes sense."

We sit, not talking, just watching the dogs until Damien's cell shatters the silence.

"Hmmm, the caller ID says Palermo's." He answers and puts the phone on speaker.

"Hello?"

"Mr. St. James, this is Giorgio. You need to pick up Lexi and her friend."

"Uh oh, what happened?"

"Four bottles of wine, sir."

"Ah. We'll be right there."

After he disconnects, he says, "You mind driving, so I can drive Lexi's car home?"

"Not at all. Let me get the dogs settled, then I'll pick you up in your driveway."

"Thanks, man."

We get inside the restaurant only to find ourselves being shouted at about how hot we are followed by boob adjustments.

"We need to get them home now," Damien exclaims.

"Ya think? Good lord!"

As we get closer to the table, the two drunkettes try to wolf-whistle at us, but all they manage to do is spit. I can't help but laugh when Mel gets up, stumbles, and falls into my arms.

"Wow, you is vewy strong," she mumbles, followed by a string of hiccups.

"And you're very drunk, my love,"

"Not dwunk, just happies."

"Okay, Miss Happypants, let's get you home."

"K, sexy cowdude."

"Can you wait with the ladies so I can pay their check?" Damien asks.

"Of course."

When Damien returns, he helps Lexi up, and we help our women attempt to walk out of the restaurant. We make it halfway before we scoop them up in our arms and carry them. I get Mel up into my truck and get her seatbelt on, then help Damien get Lexi into her car.

"Thanks, man. Talk to you tomorrow," Damien says.

"Night," I say. By the time I get in the truck, Mel's sound asleep. I drive home in silence, park in the garage, then carry her inside and right to bed.

After getting her into her pajamas, I get her settled under the covers. I run the dogs outside for their last bathroom break, then settle in bed next to my sleeping beauty. I hope Lexi got her to open up. That is if they even remember tonight.

Not long after I lie down, I feel her stirring before she flies out of bed and beelines for the bathroom. I follow her in, holding her hair as she throws up and slumps over the toilet. I grab a washcloth, run it under cool water and hold it on the back of her neck. When she's done emptying her stomach, I grab the chair from our bedroom, drag it into the bathroom and help her sit.

I hand the washcloth to her, and she covers her face.

"I'm so sorry," she whispers.

"Nothin' to be sorry for."

"What about this?" She gestures around the room.

"Angel, we all have nights like this."

"But you shouldn't have to take care of me."

"I'm your man. That's what I'm here for."

She pauses for a few moments before nodding slowly, like the words needed to sink in. "Thank you. I really need a shower." She tries to stand, but she's too weak and falls back to the chair. "Okay, maybe later," she whispers.

"Hang on." I grab a metal folding chair and set it up in the shower stall. I help Mel undress and carry her to the chair. I get myself undressed and join her. After getting the water temperature set, I detach the shower head and rinse her. After cleaning everything I can reach, including her hair, I help her stand.

"Hold on to me." She holds on for dear life while I clean her cute little bottom. Once she's all rinsed, I get her back in the chair and give myself a quick shower, then get out and wrap a towel around my waist. After handing her a towel, I scoop her up and set her down on the floor. She clings to me while I dry her off.

"Thanks, cowboy," she murmurs.

Once I finish helping Mel blow dry her hair, we climb back in bed, still naked. She snuggles close to me, and quickly falls asleep, using my chest as her pillow. I kiss her forehead and after a few minutes of listening to her breathe, I drift off myself.

I'm in the kitchen with the dogs the following morning. Mel shuffles in dressed for work. She plops down at the kitchen table.

"You look better than last night," I tease, handing her a cup of coffee.

"Did I do anything embarrassing?"

"Other than a very public boob-grab, no."

"I did what?"

"Giorgio called Damien to come get you gals. When Lexi saw us walk in, she decided the two of you needed to adjust your boobs for us."

"Oh lord," she says, burying her face in her hands. "I'm so sorry."

"Truth. It was pretty damn sexy." That gets a small laugh out of her. "Are you sure you're okay to work today?"

"Yeah. Besides, I don't wanna give Daniel any ammunition."

"Yeah, I guess. I really wanna deck that asshole. Again."

"Me too."

After managing to get a piece of dry toast down, Mel heads off to work. I take the dogs outside and see Damien and Lexi. They're standing with their backs to the fence talking and don't notice me walking over. As I get closer, I can hear their conversation.

"So, did Mel tell you anything last night?" Damien asks.

"Yeah, and it's not good."

I know I should walk away, but I need to know what's going on with my girl, so I stand and listen.

"What's up?"

"Abby's still here. And Daniel hired her as his assistant."

My jaw drops as lava courses through my veins. "What the fuck did you just say?" I shout.

Lexi and Damien both jump then turn around.

Lexi's eyes are wide and full of surprise and maybe a little fear at my outburst. "I-I-I guess Mel didn't tell you?" Lexi asks.

"No, she fuckin' didn't. What the fuck?"

"I'm sorry," Lexi whispers as tears fill her eyes. It instantly calms me down.

"Hey man, I know you're upset, but don't shout at my wife," Damien warns.

"Sorry, man. Lexi, I'm sorry. Not your fault." I give her hand a gentle squeeze.

Lexi looks at me with watery eyes. "It's cool. I told her she needed to tell you, that you had the right to know."

"Yeah I did. I'll talk to you later." I give her hand another squeeze to reassure her that my anger isn't towards her. I storm away before they can respond. Why the fuck would she keep this from me?

I get started on my work for the day, hoping to work off the aggression, but all I can think about is what I heard this morning.

By the time I'm done, I've calmed a little, but I'm still plenty angry. I hear Mel's car pull into the driveway, and I race out front. I just stand there while she gets out of the car.

"Are you okay? You look pissed," she says.

"You're damn right I'm pissed. How the hell could you keep something like that from me?"

She tilts her head, but I can see her eyes fill with realization. "Something like what?"

"You know what! I had every damn right to know Abby didn't leave!"

"Lexi wasn't supposed to tell you," she whispers, looking at her feet.

"She didn't. I overheard her telling Damien. And YOU should have told me."

"I know, and I'm sorry. I just didn't know how."

"You open your mouth and speak. Not that hard."

Mel's face falls, and I regret saying that.

"Sorry. Shouldn't have said that."

She shakes her head in acceptance of something she doesn't need from me. "I deserve it, and I deserve your anger."

Softening my tone and taking her hand, I say, "No, you don't. Well, maybe a little, but most of my anger is at Abby. Mel, we can't keep secrets, especially big ones like this."

"I know."

"So tell me, how much will you have to deal with her?"

"Too much. Daniel put her in charge of handling all of the executives. And he knows exactly who she is."

"Fuck. Maybe it's time for you to quit."

"Maybe, but isn't that letting them win?" she asks, biting her lip.

"S'pose you're right, but I hate the thought of you dealing with her."

"Yeah, me too, but I'll survive. I always do."

"I know, but baby, look at what it's done to you."

"I'm fine."

"Yeah, you keep sayin' that."

"Seriously, especially now that you know."

I sigh but choose to let it go. "Are you sure that's all?" I ask firmly.

"Yeah."

"Okay."

"Now, go get cleaned up. I'm starving."

"I'm glad your appetite is back." I kiss her head.

"Me too. I'll get something ready while you're naked and soapy."

"Or, you could join me."

"Mmmm, let's go."

I tug her to the shower.

After our shower and dinner, we're sitting on the couch watching one of Mel's favorite shows, *S.W.A.T.* I'm not convinced she loves the show as much as she loves Shemar Moore, but she claims it's the show. She's cuddled against me, while the dogs are on the floor in front of us.

For the first time in too long, I feel like I have my woman back, and it feels amazing. I hope it lasts.

Chapter Eleven

Mel

About a month has gone by since Abby started working here, and so far, I've been able to cope. Another welcome Friday rolls around, and of course the clock is dragging. Mid-afternoon, she appears in my doorway, and if looks could kill, Judd would be sleeping with a ghost.

"Can I help you with something?" I ask as sweetly as possible.

"Nope. Just checking in."

"Okay. Everything's good here."

"Are you sure?"

"Have you heard different?"

"No. Just making sure you're truly happy here."

"Absolutely. I enjoy my job."

"Yeah, well, okay."

Without another word, she turns and speed-walks out of my office. *What the hell was that all about?* I shrug it off and finish up the last of my work, then get ready to head out. Jay stops by just as I'm shutting down my computer.

"Doing okay?" he asks.

"Always. I did have a weird conversation today."

"With?"

"Abby." I fill him in on the exchange.

"Sounds like she's tryin' to get you to badmouth someone or something."

"That's what I thought, too."

"Everything good with Judd?"

"Yeah."

"I'm glad. Now, let's head out before we have to deal with anyone."

"Please."

We walk out to the parking lot. Jay gives me a quick hug before we get in our cars and head home. Jay's been spending most of his free time at the bar where Tammy works. I know he has a thing for her, but he won't admit it. I have no idea what Judd and I are doing this weekend. No matter what it ends up being, I know I'll enjoy it.

Like most days, the sexiest man I've ever laid eyes on sits on the porch waiting for me. Today, though, I can tell by the look on his face he's up to something. I race over to the porch, anxious to find out what.

"Honey, I'm home," I tease when I sit next to him.

"Cute. Now, are you ready for a big surprise?"

"Always."

"We have plans tomorrow night."

"Oh yeah? What are we doing?"

Judd hands me an envelope, and when I look inside, I scream. "Are you serious?"

"Damn right, girl."

"How'd you do this?"

"Dean knows people."

"Oh my god. I can't believe I get to see Godsmack live and do a meet and greet."

"Nothing but the best for my woman."

"This means so much to me. Thank you. This band has definitely been an important part of my life."

"How so?"

"I've never told anyone this. Not even Lexi."

"You can tell me."

"I will. I promise. After dinner, okay?"

"Yeah, of course."

After dinner, we're cuddled on the couch, and I know I can't avoid it any longer, so I take a deep breath and exhale, hoping I can keep my crying to a minimum.

"I'm ready to tell you now."

"Then I'm ready to listen, my love."

I lay my head in Judd's lap and look up at him. "You know when I found out I couldn't have kids, Doug was nasty to me. Well, he wasn't the only one. My mom, Trish, my dad. It was awful, and I was feeling the lowest I'd ever felt."

I sigh before I continue, all those awful feelings rushing back. Judd strokes my hair.

"I had recently heard Godsmack for the first time and loved it. But it wasn't the music that really changed things for me."

"What was it?"

"I was reading an article in *Rolling Stone.* The article was talking about Sully being Wiccan. At that time, I didn't know what that was, but I was curious. So, I went to the bookstore at the mall. Back when those still existed."

"Yeah, I remember those days." He gives me an encouraging smile.

"So, I went to the spiritual section and picked up a beginner's guide to Wicca. As I started reading it, something happened to me. I felt that darkness lifting; the pain I was feeling inside subsiding. It was like I was meant to hear their music and read that article."

"Wow. That's amazing. So, and please, if this is too personal, feel free to tell me, did you start to practice?"

"Well, not at first, but I did read about it. And then something else happened. Something incredible. Something that changed me forever."

Judd looks at me, but doesn't say anything.

"A couple of weeks after first reading the book, I had a dream. I was taken to this place, and when I got there, a voice told me they had been waiting for me. It's hard to describe, but you could feel magic in the air. When I woke up, I knew."

"Knew what?"

"That this was my path. But I never actually told anyone. There's still somewhat of a stigma with this religion, and I felt I had to keep it to myself."

"Nobody should ever have to feel that way, but I get it."

"So, you're okay with it?"

"I would never judge you on anything. And I would never judge anyone on their religion, so yeah, I'm absolutely okay with it."

"I love you." I sigh with relief.

"I love you. Thank you for trusting me with this. One more question, if you're up for it."

"Ask me, but I can't promise I'll answer."

"Fair enough. You don't say much about your dad. What happened?"

My chest tightens. "Can we save that for another time? It's a tough and long story, and I'm just not up for it tonight."

"Of course. Nobody understands that more than me."

I sit up and throw my arms around Judd's neck. He leans down and kisses me with a sweetness I'm not used to. Most of the time, he's trying to eat my face! My heart swells in my chest and butterflies dance in my stomach like this is the first time we've been together.

"So, baby, I have a few more details about tomorrow night."

"Oooh, I wanna know."

"Since the show's at the Hard Rock in AC, I booked us a suite. A limo's going to pick us up and take us there, then bring us home on Sunday. Lexi and Damien are going to watch the girls."

"Oh my god, Judd, you're the best. I'm so beyond excited!"

"My pleasure, love."

We watch TV a little while longer then head off to bed. I get the best night's sleep I've had in a long time.

The next morning, I'm doing my best Tigger impression while I wait for the limo to pick us up. After a delicious breakfast cooked by the world's hottest cowboy, we pack for our getaway.

After we pack Daisy and Lily's stuff, we take them next door then head back to wait for our fancy ride. When a black stretch limo pulls into our driveway, I start bouncing even more.

"Babe, if you bounce any harder, you're gonna knock yourself out with those sexy breasts."

"Oh my god, Judd!" I blush, but those words do something unholy to my insides.

He carries the bags outside with a cocky smirk on his face that tells me he knows exactly what he just did to me. Our driver takes them and puts them in the trunk, then opens the door for us.

Judd helps me in, then climbs in next to me. A bottle of Moscato is chilling along with two wine glasses. Judd pours us each a glass as we sit back and enjoy the ride to New Jersey.

I still can't believe I get to meet one of my heroes tonight. Stealing a line from one of my favorite movies, *Pretty Woman,* I say, "If I forget to tell you later, I had a really good time tonight."

Judd lifts my chin and kisses me with a passion that soaks my panties. I hope we have some time to spend in the room before the concert.

"You look so damn sexy. I love a woman in a rock t-shirt."

"You look hot no matter what. But damn, especially in those tight white shirts."

It didn't take long for those shirts to fly off once we reached our suite.

Chapter Twelve

Mel

Famished, we head down to the Hard Rock Café for dinner before the concert. When we finish, we have some time to kill, so we decide to try our luck at one of the black jack tables. After a few hands, we're both ahead, so we cash in our chips and head to Etess Arena, the concert venue located in the hotel. While we wait for the doors to open, we grab a couple of cocktails.

"I still can't believe we're in the front row," I say, starting my bouncing again.

"Yeah, and I checked the map, we're center of the row, right in front of Sully."

"Eeeek!" I squeal as an excited smile appears on my face.

"You're so damn cute, woman."

When security opens the doors, we walk inside, and an usher escorts us to our seats.

"I should go grab some merch before it sells out," I say.

"No need. I talked to Dean, and he had them put aside two of everything for us."

"Wow. You thought of everything." It's so endearing to be able to just relax and trust the man next to me to take care of it all.

"For you, anything."

As it gets closer to showtime, the crowd fills in until there's not a single empty seat. When the lights dim and the opening notes of the intro medley, Queen's *We Will Rock You,* Beastie Boys' *So What'cha Want,* Rush's *Tom Sawyer,* and Aerosmith's *Dream On,* the crowd jumps to their feet. There's nothing like that first moment.

The on-stage screen turns on, and I scream when I see the band walk toward the stage. Shannon Larkin takes his place behind the massive drum kit, followed by Tony Rombola and Robbie Merrill standing on either side of the stage.

Finally, the man comes out, and the crowd gets even louder. Sully takes his place, center stage, just as the opening notes of *Soul on Fire* starts. The entire crowd sings along. Such a magical moment.

The rest of the set list includes *Cryin' Like a Bitch, You and I, Lighting Up the Sky, Something Different, What About Me, Bulletproof, Awake, Under Your Scars, Voodoo, Batalla de los tambores,* and *Whatever.*

After a brief encore, they return and treat us to *Surrender* and *I Stand Alone.* After the last song, the band joins Sully center-stage and bows while thanking the crowd for an amazing night.

An usher then comes on stage and tells those of us who have VIP passes to stay in our seats until the rest of the crowd clears out. After the last of the crowd was gone, they close the doors of the arena, and the band joins us in the seating area. The band mingles with the VIP fans. Of course, I get hit with a bout of fan-girl shyness and am afraid to approach any of the members.

All of a sudden, I hear Sully's voice saying, "I'm looking for Mel McNeill."

My jaw drops, and my feet freeze as I forget my name. Luckily for me, I have Judd here. I snap out of it when I hear him say, "She's over here."

I watch, star-struck, as Sully makes his way to where Judd and I are standing. All I can do is giggle like a schoolgirl. Sully flashes his handsome smile at me, and I nearly faint at his feet. It takes me a few minutes to compose myself and remember that I am an intelligent, functioning adult.

After Sully chats with Judd and I for a few minutes, he calls the rest of the band over. Their manager snaps a picture of Judd and I with the band. Then yet another amazing surprise comes my way.

"We heard how much you love us, so in addition to the merch you ordered, we've included a copy of each of our CDs signed by the entire band. And you're also the lucky recipients of tonight's set list, also signed by the band and in a frame," Sully says.

A lump forms in my throat, and I fight back a scream of excitement. "Wow. I don't know what to say except thank you. You have no idea how much you've helped me over the years," I say.

"I'm so happy to hear that. We make music for the fans, so to hear that we've had that impact means everything."

The band stays with us for about an hour. After a round of hugs and handshakes, they head backstage. Judd and I take our haul up to our room.

"I'm so wired after that. You wanna hit the casino?" I ask.

"Yeah, let's go." Judd locks our merch in the room safe, then we head downstairs.

"I wanna check out the slots. Maybe just some penny slots for fun." As we're walking, I see a row of machines called *Piggy Bankin'* that look fun. We sit down and start playing twenty dollars each. After a couple of spins, I hit the bonus game and end up tripling my money.

"Damn, woman, it must be your night."

I smile. "Definitely what I needed."

"So, you gettin' tired, or are you up for some dancing?"

"Dancing sounds fun."

After we cash in our tickets, we head to Daer Nightclub, also located in the hotel.

It's almost three in the morning before we're back in our room, both of us completely exhausted.

With barely enough energy to get into our pajamas, we crawl into bed, and sleep until almost nine. Judd orders room service while I shower. After I'm dressed, he showers while I wait for the food.

After we enjoy a delicious breakfast of French toast and bacon, along with the most delicious coffee I've ever tasted, we check out and head downstairs to wait for our limo. We go outside when the driver pulls up and get in the car while our driver loads our luggage.

"I wish this weekend didn't have to end, but I'll never forget it," I say.

"It was my pleasure, my love."

I lay my head on Judd's shoulder, and the next thing I know, he's shaking me.

"Wake up, baby, we're home."

"What? How? We just left."

"You fell asleep before we were even out of AC."

I frown. "I'm so sorry."

"No need. You're adorable when you sleep. You have the cutest little snores."

"I DO NOT SNORE!"

"Uh, yeah, you do." He grins.

"Well, you fart in your sleep."

"MELISSA!"

We're both in hysterics as we get out of the limo. After dropping our bags inside, we walk out back when we hear barking. All four dogs are running around chasing a ball. Daisy and Lily catch sight of us and beeline to the fence. Damien and Lexi join them.

"So, how was it? Tell me everything," Lexi says.

"Oh my god, Sully is so nice. So is the rest of the band. We had a blast," I say.

"Did you do anything else? At least anything you can tell me."

"Shut it, dirty girl." I laugh. "We did a little gambling, then dancing at Daer."

"I'm so glad. With everything you've been through, you deserved this."

"Definitely much needed."

After we collect our dogs, we head back home.

"I could use a soak in the hot tub," I say.

"Might I join you?"

"But of course, my sexy cowboy."

After we get into our swimsuits, we head out back and get in the tub. I sit back and rest my head on the pillow as Judd turns the jets on.

After a much-needed nap, I wake up in the mood for some naughty fun. I slip my bikini bottom off and straddle my man. Pressing my body against his rippled chest, I kiss him hard, leaving no doubt what I want.

"Fuck, woman," he growls as my hand slides inside his swim trunks.

"I wanna fuck you. Damn, your dick's so hard. I need that inside me now. Get those trunks off."

He slides his trunks off, and I feel his hot skin against mine. I unfasten my bikini top, running my hands over my breasts as I slide the top off.

He licks his lips before he turns his tongue on my nipples. I grab his dick and lower my pussy down, taking every inch inside me. Water splashes everywhere as we move together. Judd meets my strokes with hard thrusts, setting my insides on fire.

"Oh, so good, cowboy."

"You're incredible, baby. Ride me harder."

"Only if you say please."

"Please, god, woman. Ride me like your life depends on it."

It looks like a tidal wave coming out of the hot tub while I fuck Judd harder than ever before. My entire body shakes as I come undone. Wave after wave of pure ecstasy consumes my body. I feel the heat of Judd's seed as he empties himself inside me, tiger-like growls coming from his throat.

He pulls me tight against him. "Baby, you never stop amazing me. I love you," he says.

"I love you so much. But now, I need you to feed me."

"I thought I just did," he says with a chuckle.

"Not with your dick, silly. I'm starving after that bounce-fest."

"You sure do bounce like a queen." Judd laughs, and I laugh with him.

After dinner, we're sitting on the couch when my cell phone rings. "Oh, shit," I say when I look at the screen. Judd just stares at me. "Hello."

"We're having a birthday party for your stepfather this Friday night. Can we expect you?"

"Do you really want me there?"

"He does."

"Then that's the only reason I'm saying yes. But I won't come alone."

"Didn't think you would."

I disconnect, not wanting to hear even one more word from my mother's nasty mouth.

"It'll be fine, sweetie," Judd says.

I sure hope he's right.

Chapter Thirteen

Judd

The day of the birthday party, I take a break to have some lunch. I see Damien, so I make a detour to the fence.

"Hey, man, how's things?"

"Mel's a bit on edge."

"What's goin' on?"

"Her stepdad's birthday's tonight."

"Oh no, don't me you're going."

"Yeah. I'm worried, especially since Trish has been quiet."

"And what if Trish invites Daniel?"

"Shit. Didn't think about that. Well, I'm definitely not letting her out of my sight. That little jerk so much as looks at her...well, would you be willing to post my bail?"

He grins. "Yeah, of course."

We both laugh, though part of me thinks I may need him.

"I hope nothing happens. Not sure how much Mel can take."

"From what Lexi says, her family has always been challenging."

"Yeah, and I think I've only scratched the surface. She never mentions her biological father."

"Have you asked her?"

"She said she would tell me some time, but it was when everything was happening with Abby, so I haven't pushed it."

"She will when she's ready, I'm sure."

"I know. I just want her to finally put all this shit behind her."

"I get it. It took time with Lexi, so just hang in there."

"Thanks, man."

"And if you two do end up in jail, Daisy and Lily can stay here," Damien says just as Lexi joins us.

"Why would you end up in jail?" Lexi asks.

"We have to go to Mel's mom's house tonight."

"Ah. Her stepfather's birthday, right?"

"Yeah."

"Brace yourself. It's an interesting dynamic."

"I'm sure. All I care about is that nobody upsets Mel."

"I get that. I hope you get to meet her aunt."

"Oh, yeah?"

"Yep, her mom's sister is awesome. She loves Mel."

"Then I can't wait to meet her."

"When Mel gets home, ask her about Aunt Mimi."

"I will. I gotta run. I have a few things left to finish before Mel gets home."

After I wave goodbye, I head back to the farm and finish up the last few things on my list for today. I decide to wait for Mel to get home before I shower. I'm out back when she gets home, so I grab the dogs and walk around to the front just as Mel's getting out of her car.

"I thought you would have been cleaned up," she says.

"I was waiting for you. I thought a nice relaxing shower then dinner would help."

She doesn't say anything. Instead, she walks over to me, throws her arms around my neck, and crushes her sweet lips to mine. Damn, I love this woman.

After we shower, I make us each a BLT on rye, and a small side salad.

Mel's quiet during dinner, and I don't push her. I know she's trying to prepare herself for tonight.

"What can I get you to drink?" I ask.

"As much as I would love something with alcohol, I need to have a clear head tonight, so just some iced tea, please."

"At your service, ma'am."

"Why, thank you, good sir."

After we finish dinner, we take the dogs out back. Mel grabs a couple of tennis balls and plays with them. Little calms her more than those two girls. And watching the three of them interact calms me. My three beautiful ladies. I would die to protect any one of them.

That gets me thinking about my father.

Instead of feeling about my mom like I feel about Mel, he decided the answer was to kill her.

I need to push those thoughts out of my head right now. I need to keep my focus on getting Mel through tonight. We have no idea what we're walking into.

I hate that I have to say this, but I call down to Mel. "We need to get ready to go."

Mel's shoulders tense up as she grabs the two tennis balls and calls the dogs into the house. She gives them each a small treat and a rub on the head. I load the Spotify app in my truck and search for Godsmack.

Trying to keep her focused on positive things, I ask, "Tell me about Aunt Mimi."

She tilts her head. "How'd you know about her?"

"Lexi."

"I hope she's there tonight. You know how Trish and I are polar opposites?"

"Yeah."

"My mom and aunt are the same way. I'm definitely more like my aunt."

"Then I know I'll like her."

"She'll like you, too. I have to warn you, though, she has no filter, and she reads a lot of romance novels."

"Duly noted," I say, laughing.

We pull into the driveway, and I see Mel shudder. "We can go home. I can tell them you're sick," I say.

"Tempting, but I won't do that to my stepfather."

"Fine, then how about a code word if you need me to get you home?"

"If I say I need to feed the dogs, I'm ready to go."

"Got it."

She jumps out of my truck, sighs, and says, "Let's do this."

Mel

I ring the doorbell, and I'm met with a nasty sneer when the door opens.

"Well, if it isn't my oh-so-lovely sister and her cowboy," Trish says.

"Don't start. I'm here to celebrate dad's birthday. Nothing more."

"Fine. Come in, your highness."

I feel Judd's breath on my ear as he whispers, "Deep breath, love."

Following Judd's advice, I walk into the living room. I give my step-father a hug. "Happy Birthday," I say.

"Happy Birthday," Judd says, holding out his hand.

"Thank you both," Dad says, returning Judd's handshake.

I hear a voice call out, "Is that my favorite niece?"

My sister sneers again, as Judd whispers, "Aunt Mimi?"

"Yeah."

"I like her already," he says with a smile meant only for me.

I give my man a little giggle just as I'm smothered by one of my favorite people. Aunt Mimi is five feet three inches of fluffiness. Her word, not mine. I've just always seen her as comforting, one of the few people who's always been in my corner.

"And who is this Adonis?" Aunt Mimi asks, as her eyes scan Judd from head to toe.

"This is my boyfriend, Judd. Judd, this is my Aunt Mimi."

"Damn, girl. You did good," Aunt Mimi shouts. She breaks into a coughing fit.

"Are you okay?" I ask, instantly concerned.

"Oh, yeah. Just a tickle, dear. Nothing to worry about. Now, tell me about that handsome hunk of beef."

My face turns bright red, as Judd flashes his megawatt smile at her. Linking her arms through mine and Judd's, she says, "Come. Tell me everything." She drags us to the kitchen, and the three of us sit around the table.

"What do you wanna know?" I ask.

"Well, I see you haven't scored any points with Trish."

"Yeah, because I won't give her money."

"Good. She's an adult. She can earn her own money."

"That's what I said."

Turning to Judd, Aunt Mimi says, "You make sure she sticks to that. This one has a heart of gold, and I don't want anyone taking advantage."

"Never on my watch."

"Good man. Now, tell me about you."

"Well, most important is that I'm crazy about your amazing niece."

"What was your childhood like?"

"Um, Aunt Mimi, how about a different topic?"

Aunt Mimi wrinkles her forehead as she looks at Judd. "It's okay, sweetie," Judd says.

He takes a deep breath and gives my aunt an abbreviated version. She puts a tiny hand on his arm and says, "I'm so sorry. I'm glad you've found comfort in this beauty."

"She's the first person I ever told. It was a weight off my shoulders, for sure."

"My sweet, quiet niece. Such a good listener, always was."

"Oh yeah, she's just Little Miss Perfect," Trish spits as she enters the kitchen.

"Jealousy doesn't become you," Aunt Mimi says.

"Jealous? Of that loser? Hardly!"

"And a liar, just like your mother," Aunt Mimi chastises.

"Aunt Mimi, you're mean. You always liked that bitch more than me," Trish says.

"You're partially correct. I have always liked Melissa more, but because she's a kind-hearted, hard-working soul who, despite how she was treated by her family, made something of herself."

"Well, she couldn't make babies like a woman should, so guess she ain't all that great," Trish says.

Tears threaten to spill, but I blink them back. I'll be damned if I'm going to let that nasty sister of mine make me cry.

At that moment the doorbell rings, and Trish bounces out of the kitchen. *Great, what's she up to now?*

Trish re-enters the kitchen and when I see who's with her, I feel like someone punched me in the stomach. I look over at Judd, and he looks pissed.

"Everyone, I'd like you to meet my friend, Daniel. Oh, actually, Mel, I guess you already know him."

"I do. Nice to see you outside of work, Daniel."

"Melissa," Daniel snaps.

Judd walks over to me and whispers, "You wanna go?"

"Hell no. I'm not letting them win," I whisper back.

Aunt Mimi motions Judd and I to the living room. "Let me guess, no love lost there?"

"Not at all. He's been giving me an awful time at work."

"I gotta say, I'm pretty pissed she invited him here. Though, not surprised," Judd says.

"You're a good man. I definitely approve, my loves."

My mother walks into the living room, a smug look on her face. "Well, I finally have a daughter I can be proud of," she says. "Unlike you with your stupid cowboy, your sister's with an educated businessman."

I'm about to respond, when Aunt Mimi stands up. She suddenly looks six feet tall. "So, Janice, let me get this straight. You have a daughter who finished at or near the top of her class in both high school and college, is an executive board member, and owns her own home. Not to mention her sweet and hardworking, *intelligent* boyfriend. And you're proud of the daughter that can't hold a job and is still living off her parents? You really need to get your head out of your ass."

"Yeah, well, I would rather have that than the ridiculous shit this one brings to the table."

73

"Then I feel sorry for you. This woman is amazing, and you don't deserve to have her for a daughter."

"She might as well not be my daughter for the little she's done for this family."

"Because she won't financially support her sister?"

"Yeah!"

"You don't know shit, Mom," I shout, finally losing it. "You have no idea some of the things I've done. Especially for my biological dad."

"Like what?" my mother snaps.

"You know what? Never fuckin' mind. I didn't do the things I did for recognition. Happy birthday, dad," I call into the kitchen. "I'm sorry about all this, but I can't be here anymore."

"Yeah, typical," Trish says. "Always running out on your family."

"Go to hell!" I shout.

"That's where you're headed!" she shouts back.

"You know nothing about your sister," Judd says. "And it's a shame. She's amazing."

"You two jackasses belong together," Trish says. "You're both assholes."

"Well, you know what they say," Judd says. "Birds of a feather fuck together."

Aunt Mimi doubles over with laughter, and I give her a big hug. She whispers in my ear, and I smile. She gives Judd a big hug and walks us to the door. "I love you both very much."

"Love you more, Aunt Mimi," I say.

She erupts into another coughing fit and takes a drink of water.

"Are you sure you're okay?" I ask, my brows furrowed.

"Honey, don't worry about me." She hugs me.

"I'm worried about her," I say to Judd when we're outside.

"Me too," Judd says as we walk out to his truck without another word.

Chapter Fourteen

Judd

"Okay, I gotta know," I say.

"What?"

"What did your aunt whisper to you when you hugged her goodbye?"

I fight a smile. "I'm not sure I should tell you."

"Oh, and why not?"

"It was about you."

"Now, you have to tell me."

"Okay, but don't say I didn't warn you. She said you have the hottest ass she's ever seen."

"That's not bad."

"Well, that's not all."

"Uh oh, what else?"

"She told me to make sure I spank it as much as possible."

"Um, oh my. She is a feisty one." A bark of laughter escapes his mouth.

"To say the least. One of many reasons I adore her."

"Well, you wouldn't want to let her down, so anytime those sexy hands want, my ass is all yours."

"Mmm, thank you, cowboy."

"Can I ask you somethin' else?"

"Of course."

"What did you mean about your dad?"

"That's part of a long story. I know I promised I would tell you someday, and I will."

"I'm here when you're ready. No pressure."

"Thank you."

We take the dogs out back when we get home and see Lexi and Damien. We all meet at the fence.

"We were waiting for a call from the police station," Lexi teases.

"Ha ha," Mel says. "But it was still eventful."

"Oh no, what happened?" Lexi asks.

"Trish was her usual charming self. Aunt Mimi was sticking up for me when out of nowhere, the doorbell rings and Daniel's on the other side," Mel says.

"I wish I could say I was surprised," Lexi says as she shakes her head.

"I'm definitely not. I knew she was gonna pull something." Mel sighs loudly.

"Yeah, I just wish it wasn't that." Lexi squeezes Mel's hand.

"Same, but you should have seen Aunt Mimi in action."

"I bet. And I bet she loves Judd."

"Oh yeah!" Mel winks at Lexi and lets out a huge yawn. "I'm sorry, I'm just exhausted after this week and tonight."

"Then tell that sexy cowboy to take you to bed," Lexi teases, and we all laugh.

After the dogs take care of their business, we head inside, and I lock up. We're laying in bed, and Mel rolls over, laying her head on my chest.

"I'm sorry about tonight."

"Baby, you have nothing to be sorry for."

"But - "

"Uh-uh. No but. I hate that you had to go through that."

"That's nothing compared to some of the other stuff Trish has put me through."

"Wanna talk?"

"I told you it was a long story, so I definitely don't have the energy to tell you everything tonight, but I feel like I owe you something."

"You don't owe me anything, but you know I'm willing to listen."

I sigh "A lot of events get us to this point, which I promise I'll tell you soon. But, my dad was in the ICU. I had already split with Doug, so Jay was with me. We were in the waiting room along with Trish and whatever boyfriend she had then. My parents had already divorced. I got turned around coming back from the ladies room and heard Trish on the phone."

"I get the feeling I'm gonna be mad again."

"Yeah, you are. She was talking to relatives that I hadn't seen since I was a kid who didn't know all the stuff that had gone on. I heard her telling them that I did nothing for him, and of course they believed her."

"And I'm guessing it doesn't end there."

"I wish. When things started taking a turn for the worse with his health, they came down to see him. I forgot to mention they live near Williamsport where the Little League World Series is played. Jay and I were finishing dinner when my dog started barking. I went to the door, and my cousin was standing there. He started lecturing me, without even giving me a chance to tell my side."

She pauses, and I can see the pain on her face.

"Jay let Midnight, that was my dog's name, out. I was standing outside talking to them. She knew I was upset. She was glued to me, and her hair was standing up. It got to the point that Jay came out and told him to leave or he'd call the police."

"Oh, sweetie, I'm so sorry."

"Just wait until I tell you the rest. But I don't have it in me tonight."

I deepen my voice, and with a smirk on my face, I ask, "But do you want it in you?"

"Oh my god, you are a horny one, aren't you?" She rolls her eyes at me.

"Can't help it when I'm next to you." I caress her beautiful face.

I wake up before my angel, so I let her sleep and sneak out to the kitchen to make breakfast. I'm feeling a bit naughty, so I decide to give my girl a thrill when she comes out. When I hear her get out of bed, I can't help but smile, as she gets closer to the kitchen.

"Damn, cowboy, watch out for bacon splatter!"

"That's what the apron's for. What else would you like for breakfast?"

"I'll take that pair of buns peeking out from that apron."

"That's what I was hoping you'd say. After I fill your sexy belly, I intend to fill up something else."

"Mmm, Judd," she says as I feel her hand connect with my naked ass.

"Seriously, though, what do you want with your bacon?"

"I could go for some cheesy scrambled eggs. I'm happy to cook if you want."

"After the night you had last night, you deserve a day of being cared for."

"Well, who am I to argue?"

"Good girl," I say with a wink. That earns me another ass-smack. Mel pours herself a cup of coffee, adds her favorite hazelnut creamer and sits down. I can feel her eyes glued to me as I cook, and my dick stirs behind my apron. I might have to take her right on the kitchen counter.

After we eat, Mel gets ready to clean up, but I stop her. "I told you today was your day to be pampered." I scoop her up and sit her on the counter while I clean up.

"Oh yeah, baby, wash those dishes for momma."

Oh, so she wants to be naughty, huh? I untie and remove the apron, and finish the dishes naked.

"Woo hoo, cowboy!" she yells.

"On your feet," I command. When she gets down, I put a towel on the counter. "Naked. Now," I rumble. It's not a request.

I watch as she removes her pajamas, and my dick's at full attention. After looking her up and down, I put her back up on the counter.

"Legs open wide," I bark sharply.

She spreads her legs, giving me full view of the prettiest pussy I've ever seen. And so damn wet. I get on my knees in front of her. My eyes drink in her beauty as I look up at her. I want a taste. I swipe my tongue between her folds, putting a little extra pressure on her clit.

"Ohhh, Judd. So good."

"Quiet. If I hear another peep, I'll stop."

After a couple more strokes of my tongue, I take her clit between my lips and suck her hard. I hear her breathing increase as her body shakes, but she manages to stay quiet.

"That's my good girl."

Her body feels like an earthquake as she explodes on my tongue. "You may make noise now," I growl against her clit, giving her the permission she silently seeks.

She screams louder than I've ever heard as her release overpowers her body. She looks like she wants to say something.

"What, baby?"

"I can't," she whispers, unsure of herself.

I'll never let that insecurity stand. "Yes, you can."

"I wanna taste."

"Of?" I raise an eyebrow in question.

"Me on your tongue."

Holy shit! I stand and crush my lips to hers. I feel her tongue twisting with mine as she moans into my mouth.

I'm aching to feel those pretty lips wrapped around my dick. After I stand, I help her down from the counter. Her legs wobble when I put her down, and she grabs my arms. We walk to the couch together, and I sit down.

"On your knees, woman. I want my cock sucked until I come down your throat."

"Mmm, yes sir."

"Good girl."

She lowers her head, taking my entire length down her throat. That never stops impressing me. I see her looking down.

"Nope. Eyes up here," I say, pointing to my face.

The sight of her on her knees, mouth around my dick, looking up at me is stunning, and I can barely control myself. I growl as her head bobs up and down in my lap and, fuck, she's so damn good at this.

"Mouth on my balls."

She sucks my balls one at a time as her tongue teases them.

"So fucking good. Now, get my cock back down that sexy throat."

I grab her ponytail, and she moans. The vibration of her lips feels so damn good. I feel myself getting close.

"Baby, you're so damn good. I'm about to come down that throat. And I better not see a single drop wasted."

I explode into her mouth. Still looking up at me, I see her throat swallow. She lifts her head and runs her tongue over my cock, cleaning up the rest of my load.

"Mmm, good cowgirl."

"Are you sure? I thought I was a bad girl." Her pretty lips form a pout.

"Oh, is that so? And what should I do with my bad girl?"

"Please put me across your knee and spank me."

"Up here. Now." I point at my lap. She lies on her stomach across my lap, and her warm skin has my dick stirring. I rub her ass, and she moans. I give each cheek a light smack.

"Mmm, harder, please."

Damn, this woman! I swat each cheek harder.

"So good, Judd." I look down, and her ass is a light red. I rub her lightly, and she moans softly.

"I love spanking my naughty little cowgirl."

"More, please."

"Damn, baby." I swat each cheek one more time. "Now, I want that sweet little pussy stretched around my cock."

She climbs onto my lap and takes me all the way inside.

"Good. Now I wanna see those tits bouncing. Fuck me hard, woman."

Holding her hips, I thrust up into her while she bounces up and down my dick. The sound of our bodies slapping is so damn hot. The scent of sex hangs in the air, and it's so intoxicating that everything around me disappears. All I can see is my beautiful woman bouncing in my lap. Watching her sends me over the edge, and I fill that sweet pussy with a huge load.

She climbs off and stands in front of me. I watch open-mouthed as she slides a finger inside her pussy, pulls it out, and slides it into her mouth.

"Mmm, you taste so good," she moans.

"Fuck, you're so damn hot. But I believe I owe you another orgasm. Have a seat and keep those eyes closed. I'll be back."

She does as she's told. I head to the bedroom and grab a vibrator out of our dirty drawer.

I kneel in front of her and put the vibrator against her clit. I turn it on full speed and hold it tight against her.

"Open your eyes and watch me pleasure you."

She opens her eyes. "Oh, Judd, that's so damn hot."

I keep it against her as she writhes and moans. Her body shakes as she has a strong orgasm, but I don't stop. I keep it pressed against her, as she comes over and over. Her body bucks as she screams.

"I'll stop if it's too much."

"No, don't stop. More, please!" Her orgasms come harder and faster until she finally pushes my hand away. I put the vibrator back.

"Use your words, woman."

"Please, too much!"

I turn the vibrator off. Her chest heaves. Her body glistens with sweat and plenty of other fluids. Her cheeks are flushed, and she can't stop shaking. She tries to stand, but her legs won't hold her up.

"You need to cool off. How about a dip in the hot tub?"

"I would if I could walk."

Without a word, I scoop her up and carry her outside. I sit her down on the edge. She swings her legs into the tub and sits down. I turn the jets on and climb in next to her laughing as she quickly falls asleep.

While she takes her much needed nap, I think of some other things to pamper my gorgeous angel.

Chapter Fifteen

Mel

I awaken, and I forget where I am for a second. Looking over at Judd, I cuddle up next to him. "Mmm, thank you for breakfast this morning. The sausage was my favorite part."

"I didn't cook sausage. I cooked bacon."

"No kidding, silly. I was talking about your nice juicy man-meat."

Judd laughs. "What am I gonna do with you, Miss Sassy?"

"Oh, I can think of some really fun stuff," I say huskily.

"I sure do love my dirty girl! And there will be time for that, but I really want to pamper you. So tell me, what would you like?"

It takes me a minute, but I finally say, "I'm embarrassed, but there is something."

"No gettin' shy now, darlin'."

"I would love to share a bath and have you wash me, including my hair."

"It would be my pleasure. That will follow a special surprise dinner I'm gonna cook for us."

"You really are the most incredible man I've ever known."

"Only because of you."

"No, I don't believe that. I think it's because of your mom."

"Thank you for saying that, angel."

"I just wish I knew if she approved of me." It's been something on my mind for a while.

"I'm sure she would."

"Maybe we'll get a sign."

Judd nods, but doesn't say anything. A sadness washes over his face, then is quickly replaced by my favorite smile.

"Well, when I was a kid, she was into butterflies. We had figurines, pictures, you name it, it had a butterfly on it."

"I love butterflies. So many different, beautiful varieties."

"Just like people. Mom always used to say that. She taught me early on to love and accept everyone for their differences."

"That's such an important lesson, and something the world still needs to get better at."

"If only people were like dogs."

"Yeah. And speaking of them, how about we head back inside and check on them?"

"Okay. Sit tight, and I'll grab towels."

Judd climbs out of the tub, and I watch his naked ass. Damn, that man is fine. He comes back and helps me out of the tub, wrapping me in a towel. I've always been an independent woman, but damn if I don't love being taken care of by my sexy cowboy. We get inside and the girls are curled up sound asleep.

"Do I get to help with dinner?"

"I thought I told you today was your day to be pampered."

"You did, but I enjoy when we cook together. Cooking relaxes me."

"In that case, I'd love the help. Would you like to put the salad together?"

"I'd love to. What are we having?"

"I'm making homemade fettuccine Alfredo with chicken."

"Yum, one of my favorites."

"I know. It's why I picked that."

Smiling at my man, I get up and start washing all the vegetables then start cutting everything up. When I finish up, I assemble everything in our salad bowl and set it on the table.

"Looks good, babe."

"Yours smells divine. Is there anything else I can do?"

"Yeah, sit that sweet little butt down and relax."

"Yes, sir."

I watch as he gets the rest of the food ready. Once he drains the pasta, I set the table and pour two glasses of wine. Judd scoops some food on each plate while I fill two small bowls with salad.

"This is by far the best Alfredo sauce I've ever tasted," I say after almost finishing the delicious meal.

"Thanks. One of Mom's recipes."

"She taught you well."

"The biggest thing she taught me, though, is how to treat a woman. So, in that vein, how about that bath?"

"Mmm, sounds perfect."

After he cleans up, Judd gets the bath ready and helps me into the tub. He climbs in behind me, and I lean back, resting against his sexy, muscular chest. He grabs my puff and shower gel, wraps his around me, and washes me.

Feeling his hands on my body drives me wild. He then washes my hair, lightly massaging my head as he goes. I feel like I'm floating on a cloud.

"Mmm, Judd," I whisper.

"I love you."

"Love you more."

After our bath, we get dressed, and take the dogs out back to play. We're sitting in the garden holding hands while the girls run laps around the yard. I feel something tickling my arm. When I look down, my eyes fill up.

"Look what landed on my arm," I say softly.

Judd's eyes glisten as he gazes at the Monarch butterfly perched on my arm. "Mom," he whispers. "This is my Melissa."

The butterfly flaps its wings, and my tears spill over. Judd holds a finger out, and the butterfly moves from my arm to his finger.

"Thank you, Momma Walker," I whisper.

"Love you, Mom," Judd says, his voice cracking. The Monarch flaps its wings once more before flying away.

Judd stands and holds his hand out. I join him, and he pulls me in tight. We stand there embracing, both of us in tears.

"I knew she'd approve of you."

I caress Judd's handsome face. "I'll never forget sharing this moment with you."

He kisses me softly, as we start swaying together. The magic I feel in this garden is like nothing else, especially after what just happened. Now, any time I see a butterfly, I'm going to know it's Judd's mom watching over us.

When it starts to get dark, we take the dogs inside and snuggle up on the couch. "I'm ready," I whisper.

"For what?"

"To tell you about my dad."

Judd pauses. "Are you sure?"

"Yeah. If I find the courage, I may even share the poem I wrote after he passed."

Judd caresses my face as I sigh and dive in.

"I know you've heard some of this already. When I was a little girl, my dad and I were close. My mom played cards once a week and when it was her turn to host, Dad would have to watch me. That's where my love of watching sports and doing puzzles came from. Then, when I was a junior in high school, there was an accident at his job."

"What did you dad do?"

"He worked at a concrete block plant. Nobody knows what happened, or at least they weren't willing to tell my mom. All we know is that he fell and suffered a head injury. We thought we were going to lose him, but he pulled through."

Going back to that time brings back a lot of pain. It takes a few deep breaths before I can continue.

"He was never the same, becoming verbally abusive toward my mom. She had enough and filed for divorce. They gave Trish and I a choice of who to live with. When she picked our mom, I felt bad and stayed with Dad. It didn't last, and part way through my senior year, I'd had enough. Of course, my mom wouldn't take me, so I moved in with Aunt Mimi."

Judd smiles softly, but I can see the encouragement behind it. "That must have been fun."

"It was, but she made me earn my keep, and I'm so grateful. I learned how to appreciate working and being independent. But we sure did have fun, especially sitting up late playing cards. She was the only one who showed up when I graduated high school."

Judd nearly scoffs. "But you were valedictorian."

"Didn't matter."

He shakes his head. "Sweetie, I'm so sorry."

"Thanks. There wasn't another thing in my life they were a part of. College graduation, wedding, my first home. All of it, only Aunt Mimi was there. And I wouldn't change it. I ran into my dad before Doug and I were still just dating, and he didn't even know it was me. He was so strung out on drugs at that point. But I still let him back in my life."

"You're amazing."

Tell my family that. They think I'm a piece of garbage.

"He eventually developed emphysema from smoking most of his life. That's why we were in the ICU the night I told you about. After the accident, he couldn't work anymore and took an early retirement. His pension and the accident settlement should have been enough to sustain him for the rest of his life, but the drugs took care of that. The only thing left was his retirement, but he was too young to use it. And Trish knew it. She also knew he didn't have a will."

"I'm not sure I wanna hear where this is going, do I?"

"Probably not, so I can stop if you'd prefer."

"That's not what I meant. I'll listen as long as you wanna talk."

Part of me is exhausted, but the other part wants everything laid out once and for all, so I keep going. "I'm sorry I have to mention Doug in parts of this."

"Not gonna lie, doesn't thrill me to hear his name, but I understand he was part of your life during some of this."

"Yeah, especially this next part. So, where my dad lived, there was a homeowner's association that included by-laws for the residents. After complaints from some of the neighbors, he was being threatened with fines."

"For what?"

"Trash in the back yard. And not the normal amount of trash. He was in no physical condition to clean up, so guess who had to do it? Doug and I took a Saturday and headed over. I can't tell you how many trash bags we filled up. The worst part, though, was the iced tea jugs."

"Expired?"

I chuckle a little because it's the only thing I can do right now. "If only. So, at that point, he had stopped paying his bills, and things were starting to get shut off, including his water. And when your water gets turned off, flushing does nothing once the water gets too low."

"Oh, Mel. You don't need to tell me what was in the jugs. What did you do?"

"Just threw the jugs in one of the trash bags. When we were done, the gloves we had on went in the trash, too. I never told anyone about any of that. I was trying to let him keep some dignity."

"Even when they accused you of doing nothin'?"

"Yeah."

"You're an amazing woman."

"Really not. Just tried to do the right thing. And trust me when I say, he didn't deserve it. When I got married, I asked him to walk me down the aisle, and he refused, wouldn't even come. I was so hurt. And that was just one of many. But yet, I was the bad person. And I know none of this compares to what your dad did."

"Baby, that doesn't make it any less awful. Our parents are not supposed to treat us like they did. But look at this way. You and I are here, thriving, both individually and as a couple."

"Thanks." I give him a soft smile and melt into him more as he holds me. "Of course, the story still isn't over. He eventually developed pneumonia. When it was clear that he didn't have much time left, I made peace with everything he had done to me, though he never actually apologized for not being there. Trish, of course, wasn't working at the time, so she was spending all day, every day with him. During that time, she convinced him that she'd done everything, and I'd done nothing."

Judd watches me, still silent, so I keep going.

"Trish convinced him to sign paperwork at the hospital to prevent them from contacting anyone but her if anything happened. So, she alone made the decision to remove the ventilator. She never gave me a chance for a final goodbye. He passed in the middle of the night, and she still didn't call me."

"When did you find out?"

"The next morning. I was in the car on my way to work. Somehow, I made it the rest of the way there. Jay took one look at me, and he drove me back home. Mr. O'Laughlin was so good to me. He gave me as much time off as I needed, and the company hired a meal service to deliver me meals for two weeks."

"That's amazing." He kisses my head. "Can I ask you something, and it's okay to decline to answer."

"Of course."

"Since he had no will, did Trish get his retirement?"

"Yep. And within weeks, blew it all. And it wasn't a small sum either. On top of it, she planned the services without me, and it was barely even mentioned that he had two daughters. Again, I kept quiet, trying to do the right thing and not make waves. By that time, Doug and I were already divorced, and Jay was my rock. I'm not sure I'd have survived otherwise."

"Nobody's more grateful than me that you did."

"The funeral was actually the day I finally knew I was going to be okay."

"How?"

"At the interment, I was sitting on the end of the row closest to the casket when I suddenly felt a hand on my shoulder. I looked back and Jay was standing behind me. Just that small show of support from a friend was what I needed. And we'd only been friends for a short time then. He always was like a big brother to me."

We sit in silence for a moment as we both process the words I just spoke. Finally, Judd breaks through the quiet. "So, you mentioned a poem. Do you still want to share? I'd love to read it, if so."

"I've never shared this with anyone. Let me go get it." I go and quickly come back. I hand a well-worn piece of paper to Judd. He's quiet as he reads my words.

Dad
  What happened to us?
  When I was little, you were my world
  Piggy-back rides, meeting the Stanley Cup Champion Flyers
  Hanging out with you when Mom had her card club over
  Staying with you when you and Mom divorced
  Why did you start using drugs?
  You missed the most important day of my life
  I wanted more than anything for you to walk me down the aisle
  But you didn't show up
  My wedding was amazing, but something was missing
  Watching Doug dance with his mother brought me to tears
  Where was my dad, where was my dance?
  The drugs cost you everything, you had no food to eat
  I couldn't let you starve
  I couldn't let you stop breathing
  So I bought you food and a nebulizer machine
  I know it wasn't much, but you hurt me very deeply
  When they took you off the ventilator, I felt so torn
  As I watched you in the hospital, you looked like a little boy
  So scared as you knew the end was near
  I know I will see you again someday
  But until then, I bid you farewell
  Please know that I really did love you and I will miss you very much.

Looking up when he's finished, I see tears in his eyes. He says nothing, just pulls me in tight. As I recall my words, a deep sadness fills my soul, and my tears spill over. As I sob, Judd's grip tightens, as if he's trying to push all the bad stuff out.

"How have you been able to be around Trish after this?"

When I finally settle, I give him an answer. "I guess I've just gotten used to it. There's still so much more that she's done to me."

"And yet, your mom expects you to help with financial support?"

"Ballsy, for sure."

"I love that you haven't given in."

"I did once or twice early on. Small amounts. But, she wouldn't stop, so I had to."

"Well, I'm proud of how strong you are. I know you don't think so, but they've put you through a lot of shit, and look at how you overcame everything."

"I'm not sure I'll ever feel strong, but being with you helps."

"I appreciate that, but you, my love, are strong all by yourself. You don't need me for that. But, I'm good for other stuff!"

"Oh, yeah? What stuff?" I smile saucily.

"You really are a naughty girl!"

I laugh. "Right now, I'm a sleepy girl."

"Then allow me." Judd scoops me up and carries me to the bedroom. It doesn't take long after my head hits the pillow for me to drift off.

Chapter Sixteen

Judd

A couple of weeks have passed since Mel told me about her father, and I'm worried. It seems to have taken a lot out of her. She's been quiet, more than usual, and just down. I'm wracking my brain trying to think of ways to cheer her up. As I'm heading inside to grab some lunch, I see Lexi in her backyard, so I walk over to the fence.

"Hey, Judd. How's Mel?"

"Still down, and I'm out of ideas."

"What about a weekend at the lake house?"

"Maybe, but I was hoping to find something I could surprise her with here."

"A stripper?" she teases.

"Lexi!"

"Sorry, just tryin' to make you smile." She pauses and her eyes widen. "Wait, I just remembered something I saw."

"What?"

"I was looking on eBay at Christmas tree ornaments, trying to find something I had as a kid, and I saw a whole collection of vintage Sesame Street ones. Mel had the whole collection as a child since that was her favorite show, but of course, her evil mother got rid of them."

"Oh wow, that would be perfect. Thank you so much!"

"Anything for our girl."

I head inside and throw a sandwich together then sit down at my laptop. I find a complete set of the ornaments and order them. I can't wait to see Mel's face when I give them to her.

I finish up lunch and head back out to the field. As I'm working, I see a butterfly near me. It lands on my arm for a few minutes then flies away. I get chills as I think about my mom. I miss her so much.

I get so engrossed in my work, I lose track of time, and I'm still in the field when I hear Mel calling my name.

My head snaps towards her voice. "Sorry, babe, I didn't realize what time it was."

"Actually, I'm glad."

"Oh, why?"

"Because we can shower together."

"I like the way you think, woman."

I smile. She seems a little more like herself today. I've been so afraid since she told me about her painful history with her dad. I still get angry when I think about what her family put her through. If I never see Trish again, it won't break my heart.

Taking her hand in mine, we head inside. She stops to pet the girls on the way to our bedroom. After a very steamy shower, we get in our pajamas and head to the kitchen for dinner.

"How does breakfast for dinner sound?" I ask.

"Yum. What did you have in mind?"

"Belgian waffles and a side of bacon."

"Oh, yes please. What can I do?"

"You wanna cook the bacon while I get the batter ready?"

"Of course."

I grab what I need to make waffle batter while Mel gets her favorite cast iron pan out of the cabinet and starts on the bacon. Of course, the dogs won't take their eyes off of her. She turns around and looks at them, and the smile on her face could light the darkest of days. She sure has done that for me.

"Less ogling, more mixing, cowboy."

I grin. "Yes, ma'am."

I finish mixing and pour the first waffle. The kitchen smells delicious. With my woman in it, it looks even more delicious.

Once the food's ready, we take everything to the table. Daisy and Lily camp out underneath, praying for something to hit the floor.

"What would you like to drink?" Mel asks.

"Check the fridge." I say, nonchalantly.

"Damn, you know what I like," she says, pulling a bottle of Dunkin' iced coffee out of the fridge with a bright smile on her pretty face.

"Look again." I flash her my best *I'm up to something* smile.

"Oooh, hazelnut creamer. I think I may have to keep you." She chuckles.

"Is that the only reason?" I taunt, hands on my hips.

"No way, my love. It would take me years to list all the reasons why I love you." She smiles softly as she gazes at me.

"My sweet Melissa." I run my fingers down her arm.

After we eat and clean up, we do our usual nightly routine of feeding the dogs and taking them out back. My jaw drops when I look out at the garden.

"Surprise!" Mel says, bouncing next to me.

"When did you do that?"

"I may have had a couple of accomplices. They picked it up and hid it in their garage. I texted Lexi before our shower, and they snuck it over."

I take a deep breath. "It's beautiful. What made you do that?"

"Look closer." I take another look at the beautiful blue iron bench. The back is the body and two large wings. The blue starts dark and lightens as you go across. My chest tightens as I gaze at my gift, and tears sting my eyes.

"Oh my god, Mel. Thank you so much. Where did you find that?"

"I was driving home from work the other day and saw a house with several benches for sale, all with different designs in the back. When I saw the butterfly, I knew it belonged in our garden."

"Thank you so much, angel. Let's go try it out." I take her hand as we walk down to the garden. As we get closer, I can see something painted on the butterfly's body. Seeing what's painted on there is all it takes for my tears to spill.

"The gentleman asked if I wanted it personalized, so I had him put your mom's name on it."

"I don't know what else to say, except again, thank you, baby."

"My pleasure."

I lean in to kiss her when we're interrupted by a whole lot of barking, followed by our dogs flying over to the fence. I don't even need to turn around. "Hey Damien, hey Lexi." We walk over to talk with them for a few minutes. "Thank you both for helping with the bench."

"You're welcome," Damien says. "Of course, this one cried the whole time," he says nodding toward Lexi.

"Hey, it was such a beautiful and touching gift, and I'm a hormonal mess."

"I know exactly what you mean," Mel adds as she and Lexi hug over the fence.

After they head home, we sit back down, and I get that kiss I wanted from the sweetest mouth I've ever tasted. After we make sure the girls do their last potties, we head to bed, and we almost oversleep.

Mel

"Shit," Mel says as she rushes around getting ready. "I'm not gonna have time for breakfast."

"Got you covered." I finish getting ready, and I'm met with a travel mug filled with hazelnut-flavored iced coffee and a sesame seed bagel covered in my favorite Philadelphia cream cheese. "You're the best," I say as I kiss Judd goodbye. I give the girls a pat on the head and race off to work.

Just as I'm coming around the corner to get to my office, I see

Daniel. *Ugh. It's too damn early to deal with the asshat.* "Good Morning, Daniel," I say, a fake smile plastered on my face.

"Melissa."

He follows me into my office. "Hope you're okay after the party."

"Oh, you mean my stepfather's birthday? No reason I wouldn't be."

"Even with everyone telling the truth about you?"

I shrug. "Nothing I can't handle."

"Your sister sure doesn't think much of you."

Nice try, dickhead.

"Is there something I can do for you? A report you need?"

"No, just checking in."

"I appreciate that. Have the day you deserve."

He turns and speed-walks out of my office. A few seconds later, Jay appears in my doorway. "Dare I ask what that was about?"

"Judd and I went to my mom and step-dad's a couple weeks ago."

"Oh, right, his birthday."

"Yeah. So, Trish decided inviting Daniel would be fun."

"Damn. That sucks."

"Yeah."

"You okay now?"

"Yep. She's done plenty worse. I also told Judd the whole sordid story about my dad. It was tough reliving some of that, but I felt a little better after I talked about it."

"I'm so glad you have him."

"Me too. Now, what about you? Anything happening with Tammy?"

"Right now, mostly just friends. I've hinted a few times about more, but she seems hesitant, and I don't want to push."

"You're such a good man. You deserve to find that special someone."

"Thanks, girl. I'm not giving up yet."

"Well, speaking of Tammy, we need another group outing."

"It's tough with her work schedule, but I'll see if she has any time off coming."

"Yay! We always have fun. We can ask Allie and Dane, too."

"Sounds like a plan. Guess I better head down to my office before you-know-who rears his slimy little head."

"Right. Lunch today?"

"I'll come grab you."

"See ya then."

After Jay leaves, I check my email and see if I have any pressing requests. I don't see any, so I start working on my standard monthly reports. A little before noon, Abby stops by. *Oh great, now I get to deal with her, too.*

"Hi Melissa."

"Hi Abby. Anything I can help you with?"

"Just checking in to see if you need anything."

"Nope, all good here."

"Okay, great."

She turns to walk out and right before she exits my office, she turns back around. "You know, you'll never be enough for him."

I open my mouth to respond, but before I get a chance, she's gone. I slump down into my chair and try to fight the feeling of dread running through my body. My stomach is in knots at just the thought of losing Judd. I hate how easy those words get to me.

I go into my bathroom and splash some water on my face. I've managed to compose myself by the time Jay gets to my office, so I don't tell him what Abby said.

After lunch, I head back to my office, but I can't concentrate. Abby's words play on repeat in my head, and I feel like I need to scream. When am I ever gonna catch a break? I just want one day where someone isn't harassing me, upsetting me, hurting me. I just want to live a quiet life with Judd and the dogs. Maybe I should think about quitting. But, if I do that, I'm letting them win. A knock on my office door snaps me out of it. I open the door, and I'm relieved to see Allie.

"Hey, Mel. Have a few minutes?"

"For you, of course."

Allie shuts the door and follows me to my desk, taking the seat across from me.

"This looks serious."

"It is, and you can't breathe a word to anyone here. And that includes Jay."

I furrow my brows. "Okay. But now you have me worried."

"I wish I could say you shouldn't be, but that's why I'm here. I caught wind of some talk that Daniel is desperate to get rid of you. And if he gets his way, you'll lose everything."

"But if I quit, same thing, right?"

"Yeah, but we do have one option."

"What?"

"Early retirement. That way, we can freeze your pension until you're old enough to receive it. Quitting or being fired, and it's gone."

I let out a breath. "I need to talk to Judd."

"I understand, but please, don't wait too long. I don't have any specifics, but I'm concerned."

"Thanks, Allie. And I promise, nobody will know you told me. But we need a cover in case Daniel sees you leave. Let me quickly finish your monthly budget and print a hard copy for you."

"Good idea."

I finish updating Allie's report and hit print. The report is just finishing when, sure enough, Daniel appears.

"What's going on here?" he asks.

"Allie needed her budget report, so she stopped down to grab it."

"Sure she did. Tell me the truth. What were you two hens clucking about?"

"I beg your pardon? We weren't socializing. Don't believe us, here's the report." I walk over and hand him the HR budget report. He huffs and thrusts it at Allie.

"Fine. But remember, I'm watching you. Both of you." He turns and stomps off like a petulant child.

"Whew, that was close," Allie says after he's gone.

"Yeah. Any more talk about this, we need to do outside of here."

"Agreed. Please talk to Judd tonight, and see if he's game for going out this weekend."

I nod, and reply, "Got it. I'll call you."

Allie nods and heads out. I slink down into my chair, and my stomach churns. Even though I talked about possibly leaving, I wasn't ready to make that type of decision yet. I wouldn't worry about my pension if it was small, but with my years of service, I stand to lose a large chunk. I know the answer, but I still feel like I need to talk to Judd first.

As if having Abby's words cycling through my head isn't bad enough, now this. I'm like a caged tiger by the time I head out. I quickly head to my car, not stopping to say goodbye to Jay or anyone else. I start up my engine and crank up Godsmack's first album, driving home with Sully's voice screaming at full volume. I sing along at the top of my lungs, and while it helps a little, I'm still feeling agitated when I pull into the driveway.

Like most days, Judd and the dogs sit on the front porch waiting for me. I didn't do a very good job hiding my feelings, but I never do with him.

"Baby, something's wrong. Sit and talk to me."

I try not to give in, but I just can't, and I look at Judd's face. The look of concern warms my heart. "Allie stopped by my office today." I fill Judd in on what she told me.

"Well, I think the answer's clear."

"It is?"

"Yeah, you need to take the early retirement. Look, I'm not gonna tell you what to do, but we've talked about you leaving and working with me here."

"Yeah, but then I'm letting them win."

"I don't see it that way. If they fired you or you quit, then they win. But this way, you don't lose your pension. You win and walk away with what you rightfully earned."

"Well, I did have that idea about what I could do here. I'd love to start selling at the farmer's market."

"Then, it's settled. First thing in the morning, go in there and retire."

"I'm not waiting that long. I just don't trust Daniel."

Chapter Seventeen

Mel

I grab my cell out of my purse and dial Allie's number.

"Hello," Allie says.

"Hey, it's Mel."

"What's up?"

"Judd and I talked. I'm going to retire. What do I need to do?"

"You have access to work from home right?"

"Yep."

"If you logon and go to the HR section, you'll see the instructions on how to submit a retirement request."

"Okay, I'll do it now. And what about tomorrow?"

"Just come in as you normally would. As soon as I process the request, I'll come down, and we'll go over everything."

"They can't deny me, can they?"

"No. You have more than twenty-five years of service, so you're eligible."

"Thanks, Allie."

"You're welcome. I'll talk to you tomorrow."

I disconnect and put my phone away.

"How do you feel?" Judd asks.

"Truth? Relieved. Nervous. Excited. I'm a little bit of a hot mess."

"Not at all. It's a big deal. But now we can get started on our next chapter."

"That's the part that has me excited."

We head inside and log on to the company network. While I'm working on that, Judd goes down to his office. I'm just finishing when he comes back, a big smile on his handsome face.

"Okay, what were you just up to?" I ask.

"I have a surprise for you. I know you have to go into the office in the morning. But the following morning, we have an appointment."

"Where?"

"You'll find out."

"Oooh, that's so mean. You know I have the patience of a small child."

"I know." His sexy smile widens.

"I'll get you back for this."

"I welcome the challenge. Now, about tomorrow. How about after you and Allie are done, I come help you pack, then we can go out to celebrate?"

"That sounds perfect. How about some dinner, now? I'm starving."

"I can think of a few ways to feed your hunger, woman."

"Mmm, Judd. I want that, but first, I need some fuel. I can't ride you without it."

We both laugh. I can't help but notice this is the best I've felt in quite some time. I don't think I realized how much all this stress at work with Daniel and then Abby was affecting me. But now, I can put it all behind me and move on. After dinner, I'm desperate for Judd to satisfy another hunger. I whisper something in his ear, and he runs to the bedroom.

After one hell of a romp in the bed, we get dressed and go sit out in the garden while the dogs play. Not long after we get out there, Dave and Maggie are at the fence barking.

"Why don't you bring them over and hang out for a bit?" Judd calls to Damien and Lexi.

Damien opens the gate and the dogs race into our yard, followed by Lexi. Damien closes the gate and they head over and sit on the other bench.

"You look especially happy," Lexi says to me.

"I have some pretty big news," I say.

"Oh, do tell," Lexi says, leaning forward.

"I filed early retirement papers at work." I can't help but smile.

"What? Why?" Lexi's mouth gapes.

"You remember my former assistant Allie?" I ask.

"Yeah." Lexi nods her head up and down.

"She moved into HR, and she got wind that Daniel is trying to get rid of me. If I quit or get fired, I lose my pension. But if I take early retirement, I won't lose anything. She risked a lot telling me."

Lexi's speechless. "Well, you seem happy." Lexi says when she's finally able to speak.

"I really am. I don't think I knew how much stress I was actually under. But I feel like a huge weight has been lifted off of me." I take a deep breath and exhale loudly.

"What's next?"

"We've started talking about some stuff, but nothing concrete yet. For now, I'm just going to enjoy it." I smile.

Lexi jumps up and claps. "We need to celebrate."

"I'm taking my girl out to dinner tomorrow night to celebrate. Would you like to join us?" Judd asks.

"Yes, join us, please," I say.

Lexi looks at Damien who says, "We'd love to."

"Great. How about six tomorrow night?" Judd says.

"Perfect," Damien says.

Lexi and Damien stay for a little while, all of us amused watching the dogs play. Dave is a total stud, and he loves having three chicks follow him around the yard. After they head home, we take our girls inside. They curl up together and quickly fall asleep, while Judd and I sit on the couch.

"Are you sure you're okay with all of this?" Judd asks.

"I wasn't sure I would be, but now that it's happening, I really am.

It was stressful enough having Daniel there, but then - " I stop short, not sure if I should mention Abby.

"Abby," Judd finishes for me. He always reads me so well.

"Yeah."

"I've been wanting you to leave, but I would never have forced or pushed you."

"I appreciate that. I think I would have been resentful if you did. I needed to get there when I was ready."

"I never had any doubt you would. You're one of the most intelligent women I've ever known."

I blush. "Thank you. That means so much."

"And you know how hot I think you are, especially in those glasses."

I snuggle up against my cowboy, loving how amazing I feel in his muscular arms. We sit quietly just holding each other, an absolutely perfect moment. I look up at him and whisper, "I love you so much."

"I love you, baby."

I try to fight back a yawn, but I'm exhausted.

"How about we head off to bed? You have a big day tomorrow."

"Sounds divine."

"And I'll be sending you off with a special breakfast in your tummy."

"Mmm, I love when you cook for me."

"I love when you cook for me. In the bedroom, that is."

I laugh. "We'll have plenty of time for that."

"And I intend to take full advantage of that."

After we get ready and climb into bed, Judd pulls me in tight. I feel so relieved and relaxed that I remember little after he kisses me goodnight.

The next morning, he lightly shakes me awake. I grab a shower, and when I come out, the house smells delicious. I get to the dining room table and see a plate with two slices of French toast covered in fresh strawberries and whipped cream.

"Wow, that looks delicious."

"You know, I have some strawberries and whipped cream left. We could have some fun with those later."

"Oh, hell yeah!"

Judd takes a swipe of his whipped cream and puts it on my lip, then leans in and licks it off. If I didn't have to be at work, I would rip my clothes off right here at the table.

"Just a little preview for later."

"I can't wait. Can we cancel dinner?"

"No, no, baby. You'll be a good girl and wait until we get home."

"Mmmm."

After I finish my breakfast, I head out, eager to sign my paperwork and pack up my office. I'm dreading one thing. I hate that I have to spring the news on Jay. I'm gonna miss seeing him every day, but this is what's right for me.

When I get off of the elevator, Allie's waiting for me. "I have your paperwork ready, so I thought we could get this done first thing before anyone gets wind of it."

"I agree."

Allie and I sit down at the small round table in my soon-to-be former office, and she opens the folder she was carrying. "I'll run through this with you, but I want to get your signature on it before Daniel finds us and tries to pull something." She turns to the last page and hands me a pen. I sign and date the form then Allie goes over each page with me. We're just finishing up when Daniel and Abby appear.

"Let me handle this," Allie whispers.

"Don't you two have work to do? This isn't a damn social hour."

Allie stands and walks over to Daniel. "Well actually, we were working."

"Oh. Well, what's in the folder?" Daniel asks.

With a smug smirk on her face, Allie announces, "Ms. McNeill informed me of her intention to take an early retirement. We just finished signing the paperwork."

"Well, I don't have to honor the request," Daniel says.

"Yes, you do. It's corporate policy. She has exceeded the required years of service. You aren't able to deny her. Ask you uncle."

Daniel rolls his eyes at Allie and pulls his phone out. His face is bright red by the end of the call. "You win this time, bitch, but I'll get you."

"Good luck, Daniel." I don't say another word. Instead, I just walk over to my desk and start gathering up my personal belongings.

Daniel and Abby storm out, and Allie heads out to file my paperwork. I'm partway through packing when I see Jay in my doorway. A lump lodges in my throat as I try to find my words.

"I don't wanna know what's going on here, do I?" Jay asks as he walks to my desk.

"Um, I don't know how to tell you this."

His expression darkens slightly. He knows something's up. "Come on, I'm one of your best friends. Just tell me."

"I retired."

"What happened?"

I wag my finger at him so he leans in closer. "It's a long story," I whisper.

"Okay, call me later and fill me in."

"Will do."

Just as Jay's leaving, I see Judd coming in. Jay stops to shake his hand. "Take good care of my friend," he says, a hint of sadness in his voice.

"Hey, sweetie. Poor Jay." He glances over his shoulder at Jay.

"Yeah, I feel bad leaving him like this."

"I know. I love the way you care about other people."

"Thanks."

"How much do you have left?"

"Everything is gathered up. I was just waiting for you to bring me the boxes."

"What else do you have to do?"

"I just need to call a tech to come get my equipment, then stop by security on my way out to turn in my badge. Allie's already been here and gone, so my paperwork is all set."

"Great. I was thinking we could stop home and drop your stuff off then make some sandwiches and take the girls to the park."

"That sounds like a perfect afternoon."

Judd's taping up the last box when Daniel and Abby darken my doorstep yet again. Judd's shoulders tense up as soon as he sees her, but he doesn't say anything.

"Just came to see if you were gone yet," Daniel says. He scowls at me.

"Almost, then the office is all yours," I say, a huge smile on my face.

"We won't miss you," Abby adds. She fixes her glare on me.

"Thank you," I say with a little extra cheerfulness.

Judd grabs two of the three boxes and starts heading out. He stops when he hears Daniel start talking.

"I've never been happier to see someone leave. The only regret I have is not firing your worthless ass when I had the chance."

Judd's about to respond when I storm over to Daniel. "I've held back in an effort to remain professional, but I don't have to do that any more. You are a complete and total asshole and an embarrassment to your uncle. He always made me feel welcome, that I had worth, and he never treated me any differently because I'm a woman. But you have done nothing but harass me since you first walked into my office. Well, now I can tell you what I've wanted to since day one. Go rot in fucking hell, asshole."

He stands there, jaw hanging open, as I return to my desk and call a tech to come grab my equipment. I grab my last box and walk with Judd to the elevator. Daniel tries to follow us, but Judd shoots him a look, and he backs off.

We make a quick stop at security. I turn in my badge, and shake hands with the guards that have been there even longer than me. They wish me well. I smile, and head out, a sense of freedom overwhelming me.

Judd loads my boxes in the backseat of his truck, He walks me to my car and, ever the gentleman, helps me in.

When we get home, I change while Judd packs a picnic lunch for us, as well as treats and water for the dogs. We load the dogs in his truck and head to the park. He turns on Spotify and brings up a special playlist he made for today, starting with *Take This Job and Shove It*. We laugh the whole ride, and other than leaving Jay and Allie, I'm feeling nothing but joy.

When we get to the park, we find an empty picnic table, secure the dogs' leashes around the table legs and sit down to eat. The weather is splendid, bright blue skies with not a cloud in sight, and a temperate seventy degrees. The girls sniff a little bit, then lay down. Judd fills their bowl with water and puts it near them.

He takes a sandwich out of the basket and hands it to me. "Chunky peanut butter and mixed fruit jelly."

"Yum, one of my favorites. Did you pack the Fritos?"

"Of course. Here you go," he says, handing me the bag.

I open my sandwich and cover the jelly with chips then put it back together. Judd shakes his head at me.

"I can't believe you never did this as a kid," I tease.

"I never heard of it."

"Wow. I wouldn't eat PB and J without chips on it."

"Well, I'm feeling a bit daring today, so let's give it a whirl."

"You'll love it." I smile as I watch Judd cover his jelly the same way I did.

He hesitates for a moment then takes a big, crunchy bite. His eyes widen. "Wow, that really is good."

"See, told ya!" I smile and bounce in my seat.

After we finish lunch, Judd runs the basket back to the truck. When he returns, we take the dogs for a walk around the park, stopping at the dock.

"I could get used to this. Though, I am looking forward to what's next."

"And I know what's next. That call I made the other day was to Art, who handles renting booths at the farmer's market."

"Oh yeah? Does that mean what I think it means?" I clasp my hands under my chin.

"We have a meeting with him tomorrow morning to go over everything. I wanted to surprise you, but I can't keep it quiet anymore!"

"Oh my god. I'm so excited." I bounce up and down.

"Of course, that's not the only surprise, but the rest you will have to wait for."

"I suppose I can handle that." I sigh.

"You don't have a choice." He sticks his tongue out at me.

"Well then, that's how you wanna play, huh?" I roll my eyes at him.

Judd laughs as he sticks his tongue out at me again.

"Oh, real mature. Though, I can think of somewhere I'd love to feel that." I bat my eyelashes at him.

"I promise you will later." He leans in and deepens his voice. "I want to taste you, baby."

I lean in and crush my lips to Judd's, leaving him no doubt what I want. He groans into my mouth as my tongue finds his. His fingers weave their way into my hair as we kiss until we're interrupted by a loud throat clearing. We turn and see Mikael and Hannah standing on the dock grinning at us.

"Playing hooky, girl?" Hannah asks. She wags her finger at me.

"Permanently. I took an early retirement." I hunch my shoulders. "Long, sordid story, but I had no choice."

"Really?" Hannah raises her eyebrows.

"Yeah. It was the only way I could keep my pension, and there were rumblings that Daniel wanted to get rid of me." I lower my head and stare at my feet.

"He sounds like a real asshole," Mikael says.

"He is. And nobody gets to treat my girl like that," Judd adds. He drapes his arm around me.

"Totally. I'd never let anyone get away with talking bad about Hannah," Mikael says. He takes her hand in his.

I let out a soft moan. "Awww, such cinnamon rolls," I say.

Hannah furrows her brow. "Cinnamon rolls?" she asks.

"Yeah, it's my favorite romance trope. The male lead is a sweetie, but still a dirty animal in bed." I smile wide.

"Oooh, I like that. I know for sure I enjoy Mikael's icing," Hannah says, as she smirks.

"Oh, hell yeah. Judd's is pretty damn good, too." I sweep my hand across my forehead.

"Good lord, girls," Mikael says. He shakes his head back and forth.

"Oh, you know you love it," Hannah says, and we all laugh.

"Well, we gotta head back to the shop, so we'll let you two get back to kissing," Hannah says. "Enjoy your retirement." She gives me a big hug before they head off.

I smile at my sweet friend. "Thanks, girl."

We sit on the dock watching the water for a bit. The girls start to get rammy, so we head back to the truck and take them home. We let them play out back until it's time to get ready for dinner.

As we're backing out of the driveway, I say, "Hey, you never told me where we were going to dinner."

"You'll find out."

"You and your surprises!"

"Because I love you more than life itself."

"I love you so much."

Judd pulls into the parking lot at BYOB, and I figure out what he's up to. There's only a few vehicles in the lot, all of which I recognize.

"You're amazing."

"Wasn't me."

"Lexi?"

"Yeah."

As we're approaching the door, Lexi opens it, and I can see she's holding something. She puts a sash on me that says Retired Queen. Damien stands, holding an open box. Lexi reaches in, pulls out a crown, and places it on my head. Judd takes my arm and links it through his. I look around and see our friends. Jason and Allie run up and smother me.

"Lunch just isn't the same without you," Jay says.

"Yeah, I miss seeing you every day," Allie says.

"It's only been one day! So, tell me. How's Daniel been?"

"He's been quiet, which honestly worries me. He's up to something," Jay says.

"He already has someone else in your role, I think an old college friend," Allie adds.

"That fast? To me, that's more proof he was planning to get rid of me."

I make my way around the room, making sure I greet everyone.

Cassie and the kitchen staff bring out several trays of food and put them in chafing dishes. Judd escorts me to the food, and I grab a plate of baked ziti and a salad. After everyone eats, Cassie rolls a cart out with a huge cake.

There's a picture of a blonde woman sitting in a hammock in the corner, and written in orange icing is 'Congratulations, Mel'.

After everyone enjoys dessert, Damien fires up the Karaoke machine, and we all take turns belting out a variety of tunes.

The party starts to wind down around eleven. There was so much food and cake left that everyone gets to take some home.

When we get home, Judd puts our leftovers in the fridge while I go into the bedroom to change. Before I even get a chance to finish, he's standing in the bedroom with the whipped cream and strawberries left from breakfast this morning.

"Naked, and on the bed." His voice is soft but sharp.

I quickly strip and lay down, my pussy wet and throbbing for my sexy cowboy. He walks over and slowly strips while I watch. I can barely contain myself when he slips his briefs off, and his cock springs to life. Fuck, I need him inside me.

Judd takes the can of whipped cream and, starting between my breasts, draws a line down to my belly button. He lines the whipped cream with pieces of strawberry.

"Lie perfectly still, woman, or I stop."

"Mmmm."

He lies down next to me and works his way down, eating each piece of strawberry as he licks the whipped cream off of me. Every inch of me wants to writhe, but I do as he told me.

When Judd's done with the last bit of whipped cream, he takes a piece of strawberry and slides it through my folds before popping it in his mouth.

"Tastes so good, baby. Now, get those legs open wide. I wanna look at that sweet pussy." I do as I'm told. He leans his head between my thighs and gazes at me. "So fuckin' pretty."

He moves his head closer to my pussy, and I feel his tongue slide into my folds as he sucks on me. The pleasure his tongue brings sends me bucking off the bed as I moan.

"Feels so good," I moan. I feel his tongue swirling my clit. "Mmm, I want you to bite me."

"Damn, woman," he says. I feel his teeth lightly nip my clit.

I arch off the bed. "Fuck, so good. Oh god, Judd, suck on me."

His lips suck me hard. The feel and sound of what he's doing to me sends me into orbit, and my entire body quakes as I scream.

Judd lays on his back. "On top of me."

Not completely down from my orgasm, I scramble to straddle my man, quickly taking him inside me. He pulls me down against his chest and wraps his arms around me. He holds me tight as our bodies move together. I love the feeling of his huge cock sliding in and out of me, setting my body on fire.

"Oh, my sweet Melissa, I love how it feels when I'm inside your beautiful body. I love you, baby."

"Mmm, so good, Judd. I love you." We keep rocking together until I feel him explode inside me. I sit up, angling my body so my clit rubs his dick as he finishes me off with an even stronger orgasm.

He pulls me back against him, our bodies soaked with sweat. Our lips meet in one of the most tender kisses I've ever felt. We kiss slowly for a while. There's just something so special about the intimacy of kissing someone that curls my toes. I love how his tongue feels on mine.

After a quick cleanup, it doesn't take either of us long to fall asleep.

Chapter Eighteen

Mel

"You know, jeans and sneakers are so much better than dress clothes and heels," I say while Judd and I enjoy a leisurely breakfast.

"You look good in anything, but I will admit, I prefer this look, too. Well, actually, my favorite look is naked, but this works."

I see Judd gazing at my exposed belly button. I went with a black-and-white checkered blouse tied in a knot at the waist, exposing just a small amount of skin. Apparently, though, enough to get my cowboy's tongue wagging. And I know exactly where I want that tongue. But right now, we have other things to focus on.

"What time are we meeting with Art?" I ask.

"Eleven. He'll be waiting at the stall for us."

Art handles all the booth leasing for our local farmers' market. I'm so excited to start this new chapter in my life. I loved my job and until Daniel came into the picture, loved where I worked. But, things change, and as I'm discovering, this is definitely a change for the better. I'll have more time at home with Judd and the dogs, plus doing something that's always been a passion of mine.

Despite being a Wednesday, the market is crowded when we get there.

"Wednesday is Senior's Discount Day, so a lot of the retirement communities rent buses. We see large groups throughout the day," Art explains.

"Are there other days that draw one demographic over another?" I ask.

"I have a guide," Art says.

"Perfect, thanks."

"Now, let's get down to business," Art says. He and Judd take a seat at a small table while I check out the booth, jotting notes in my brand new fancy notebook with my fuzzy pink flamingo pen. I have a secret addiction to office supplies. Running a business will give me a perfect excuse to do some serious shopping.

After Judd's done signing all the papers, we stop by Garden of Eden for a quick lunch before we head home.

"Time to put those organizational skills to work, my love," Judd says.

"Yeah, I want to get all of our plans written out. First thing on my mind is advertising. We need people to know we exist."

"Any ideas?"

"I was thinking we could start with a giveaway."

"What kind of giveaway?"

"Well, the street fair is this week, so I was thinking if there was still space available, we could set up a table and give away sample meals. I can create fliers to include with the meals letting people know who we are and where to find us."

"That's a great idea."

"Thank you! I just need to find out who to call to see if I can get a table at the fair."

"I can help with that," Eden says as she drops our food off. "Let me grab you the info."

"Thanks," I say.

Eden comes back and hands me a paper with a name and phone

number. "I'm pretty sure they have a few empty tables. What are you planning to sell?"

"Actually, we're not. We're doing a giveaway." I fill her in on our idea.

"That should work well. I did something similar when I opened this place."

"I can't believe this is actually happening." I bounce in my chair.

"I gotta say, this new chapter looks good on you. It's the happiest I've seen you, other than when you look at your cowboy." Eden gives me a big hug.

"We're all very lucky women. Our men are some of the best I've ever known."

"Why, thank you," Johnny says as he walks over to join us.

Eden looks up at him, and the adoration in her eyes is so sweet. They stay and chat for a few more minutes, then head back to the counter.

We're sitting at the dining room table after we get home from lunch huddled in front of my laptop, organizing our business plans in a notebook app.

"I'm gonna call quick and make sure we can get a table for this week," I say.

"Okay. Then we can plan what we want to make."

I secure our table, and we get back to planning, this time focusing on the meals we want to make for the fair. Once we have the menu set, I head to one of our local price clubs to grab what we need. I turn the corner heading toward the meat when I come face to face with Abby.

"Well, well, well, if it isn't the cowboy's sloppy seconds."

"You have no idea what you're talking about. Judd loves me."

"No, he tolerates you. I'm the only one he ever truly loved."

"Oh, right. He loves the girl that turned on him over the one who's loved and supported him."

"You just keep telling yourself that. But you'll see." She turns and walks away.

As secure as I feel in my relationship with Judd, I'm not gonna lie. Her words have me rattled and afraid. I don't think I could handle losing that man, and I sure don't wanna find out. I hate how easily she gets to me.

Turning my focus to the task at hand, I finish my shopping, pay for my order, and head home. Cooking helps calm me, so I do some prep work with the intention of spending Saturday and Sunday cooking.

By the end of Sunday our entire garage fridge is full, but we got everything to fit. Monday morning, we load everything up and head down to the fair. By lunch time, all of our meals are gone, along with our fliers. Now, if this turns into business for our market stall, we'll be in great shape.

Tuesday morning, I'm sitting out back with the dogs. My mind is a mess. Judd and I realized quickly as we prepare for our new venture that our kitchen is not enough to support the demand for our products. I'm wondering what we're going to do while Judd's out getting more hay for his horses. When he gets home, he joins us in the backyard.

"Baby, guess what?" Judd asks, as he rocks on his heels.

I bite my lip. "What's going on?" I ask.

"I found the solution to our kitchen problem."

"Wow, really. What?" My voice goes up an octave.

"The owners of a catering company retired, and their property is for sale."

"That's amazing!" I jump up and throw my arms around Judd.

"I was hopin' you'd say that. Please don't be mad, but I put a deposit down, so nobody snagged it."

"Why would I be mad?"

"Because we didn't talk about it first."

"I don't mind at all. I'm just excited to see it."

"Well, let's go."

We load the dogs up in the truck, and Judd drives us to the property. Other than some minor updates needed, the place is in amazing shape.

"Oh, Judd, this is so great. I'm gonna be able to make so much food in here."

"But, angel, you can't do this alone."

"Watch me." I stand with my hands on my hips.

"Look, I know if anyone's capable, it's you, but think how much more we could do with some staff." I stand up straight, my chin pointing up.

I tilt my head from side to side. "You're right."

"Could you put that in writing?" Judd teases.

"Ha, ha, cowboy. Seriously, though, I've had so many comments, especially from seniors, how helpful our meals are, so I'd love to make more."

"Now, we just need to find some good people."

I nod. "Maybe Eden can help me with recommendations."

"Great idea." He touches my forearm. "This way, too, you're still using your degree, my amazing woman."

"I don't know what I'd do without you." I place my hand over my heart.

He hugs me tight. "Well, you're never gonna find out."

"I'm holding you to that."

My words may sound confident, but I'm definitely not feeling that way. I'm still haunted by Abby's words. I know I should tell Judd, but I don't want to upset him. Why the hell won't she just go back to Texas where she belongs?

Judd and I spend the rest of the week getting our booth set up and starting to interview for our kitchen staff. At Eden's suggestion, we're holding a job fair on Friday. I'm anxious to get things moving, so I really want to find our entire staff this week. We take a quick break during our setup and grab a quick bite at one of the other market stands. As we're sitting and eating, I look at Judd.

"So, what happens once winter comes? The market will be closed, and you won't have much to do on the farm."

"Oh, that's easy. Lots of cuddles with my sexy woman on the couch. Or in bed. Or wherever you wanna get naked."

"Nothin' better than some hot, sweaty sex on a cold, winter day. Especially in front of the fireplace."

"Now you're talkin' my language, babe."

"Ugh, I'm gonna be sick."

We look up and Daniel, Trish, and Abby are standing there. Those lovely words, of course, were courtesy of Trish.

"Can you leave us the hell alone?" Judd asks.

"What fun would that be?" Daniel asks.

"If tormenting other people is your idea of fun, you need to get a fucking life," I say.

"That's rich coming from someone who retired and lost her chance at easy street," Abby says.

Daniel flashes her a look but doesn't say anything, and Abby looks down at her feet. He quickly pulls Trish and Abby away. Judd and I sit, dumbfounded, watching them have a hushed but heated conversation on the other side of the eatery.

"What the hell?" Judd asks.

"Got me. Sounds like they may be up to something at O'Laughlin. I'm more and more glad I got out when I did."

"Me too."

My already hot mess of a brain has something new to spin about. What the hell is going on? I shouldn't, and truly don't, care, but I'm sure curious. I'm generally a kind person, and I don't hold grudges, but I do hope that if Daniel's up to no good, he gets caught.

I shake my head, trying to clear it, so I can focus on what's truly important.

Chapter Nineteen

Judd

"Hey, doll. Are you all set for today?" I ask.

"Yes. Eden's going to meet me there and help me interview. She has a much better idea of what to look for."

"That's great."

"I definitely appreciate the help. Once we're done, I'd like to have them over for dinner to say thank you. Though, I'll be nervous cooking for a professional like her."

"Hey, don't sell yourself short. You're a great cook."

"Maybe, but I'm not at Eden's level."

"You don't have to be."

"My head knows that."

"I'll just have to keep reminding you."

"Please do. It's just hard. Every time I start to feel a little bit of self-confidence, my mind rushes back to my youth and being told repeatedly that I would never amount to anything."

"Your mom?"

"And Trish."

"Well, look at you and how your life's turned out. Then look at theirs. Trust me, baby, you're incredible and you need to hold your head up high."

She throws her arms around me. I pull her tight against me and kiss the top of her head. "I promise I'm trying to get better at believing in myself."

"I know you are. I've definitely seen a change in you since we met."

"That's because of you."

"No, doll, it isn't. I may have helped you find your confidence, but there had to be something to find."

"You really are the sweetest man."

And this man wants to be your husband. I never thought I'd feel that way again after what Abby did, but the longer my relationship with Mel lasts, the more I'm sure.

What especially strikes me is how she hasn't once mentioned marriage. Little strikes fear into the heart of even the strongest man more than being pressured or given an ultimatum. And with Mel, there's not been even the smallest hint of that.

"So, what's on your agenda while I'm at the kitchen today?"

"No special plans. I have a little bit of harvesting to do. Plus, I want to change the hay in the horse stalls, but other than that, I'll probably just hang with the dogs waiting for you. Which reminds me, any thoughts on what you wanna do tonight?"

"I have a feeling I'll be exhausted, so how about a movie night?"

"Hmm, sitting on the couch, my woman cuddled up next to me. Why would I wanna do that?" I drawl.

"Hey!"

I tickle her tummy, eliciting a loud snort-laugh. "You know I'm just teasing."

"You better be."

"And if I'm not?"

"Then my panties stay on."

"You may wanna rethink that. That's not punishing just me."

She purses her lips adorably. "Good point. Well, then I guess I'll have to give you a nice little spanking."

"Yes, please, woman."

After Mel leaves, I wait a bit then head to the next town over. I don't want anyone to see me at the jewelry store. I really want this to be a total surprise for Mel. I like Lexi, but I'm not sure she'd be able to keep this secret.

Nobody else is in the store when I walk in. I must look like a nervous wreck by the way the saleswoman speaks to me.

"I know this is a big deal. And very scary. I'm here to help make it a little less stressful. My name is Angie."

"Thank you. I'm Judd."

"A pleasure. Why don't you start by telling me a bit about your significant other?"

"What do you want to know?"

"Tell me her taste in fashion."

"She likes things simple. Jeans and t-shirts are her go-to."

"Okay, so we don't want to go with anything overly fancy. Let's start with some of our solitaires."

Angie walks me over to one of the cases and takes a tray out. My eyes scan the tray when, suddenly, a lump forms in my throat. I point but am unable to find my words.

"The butterfly?" Angie asks.

I nod yes. The body of the butterfly is made of four small diamonds. Each wing features a sapphire, and it's stunning.

"There's special meaning behind that one, isn't there?"

"Yes, ma'am. My mother, who I lost as a small child, loved butterflies."

"Then, this is definitely the one. Shall I box this up for you?"

"Yes, please."

"Would you like to pay in full today, or sign up for a payment plan?"

"I'll pay today. I plan on proposing soon."

"Wonderful. Follow me down to the computer, please."

I follow Angie to the end of the counter. She's entering the information about the ring into her computer when she suddenly looks up. "There's a very unhappy looking woman staring in here at you, sir."

I turn around, and there's Abby standing there, a scowl on her face. "My ex."

Angie nods and gets back to her work. We both look toward the door when we hear the bell chime.

Abby storms over. "What the fuck is this?"

"None of your concern, that's what."

"Ma'am, please watch your language, or I'll need you to leave," Angie says.

"Please shut the hell up, bitch," Abby says.

"Abby, you owe her an apology," I say with exasperation. I'm fed up with her.

"I don't owe shit to anyone. Well, except maybe some pay back to *Melissa* for stealing you."

"I'm not having this discussion here. Please, just leave us alone."

Abby's about to say something when Angie returns with a security guard. I hadn't even seen her leave.

"Ma'am, I'll need you to vacate the premises," the security guard says to Abby.

Abby crosses her arms across her chest. "And if I don't?"

"The police are on their way."

"Well, I don't believe you, and I'm not fucking leaving until I've said my piece."

"And are you going to tell the truth? That you broke things off with me twenty years ago? I want nothing to do with you. Please just leave us alone, especially Mel."

I see a police car pull up in front. The two officers enter the store and approach Abby. "Fine, I'll fucking leave. Mark my words, Judd, this isn't over. Your precious little girlfriend better watch her back."

Abby storms out. One of the officers walks over to me. "Sir, I'd suggest the possibility of filing for a protective order, if not for yourself, then for your girlfriend."

"Thank you. I'll speak with my lawyer. I apologize to all of you for this scene." I turn to Angie. "I'll understand if you no longer wish to sell me a ring."

"This was in no way your fault. If you're still interested, I'd love to complete the sale. Melissa is a very lucky woman."

"Thank you." I let out a relieved breath.

The officers leave, and the security guard returns to the back while Angie finishes entering the sale into her computer. After I give her my information and hand her my credit card, she processes the payment.

"What color box would you prefer?"

"Do you have black?"

"Yes. One moment." Angie takes my ring to the back. When she returns, she hands me a black felt box. She also hands me a heart-shaped box with Godiva on the lid.

Mel might love the chocolate even more than the ring.

"A small gift as our congratulations on your upcoming engagement."

"Thank you. Mel loves her sweets. I was just thinking, she may love the chocolate even more than the ring," I say, smiling.

Angie laughs as she puts both boxes into a bag. "Congratulations, and best of luck on your upcoming engagement."

"Thank you again for your help today. One question, if I may."

"Of course."

"Do you have a wedding band that will work with this ring?"

"Yes, we have several. When you're ready, I'll be happy to help you."

"Wonderful. I'll definitely be back."

"Have a great day, Mr. Walker."

"You as well."

I head out to my truck, placing my bag on the passenger seat. Now, I need to decide how and when I want to propose.

When I get home, I hide the ring and the box of candy in my safe so Mel doesn't accidentally find it. After I check on the horses and change out their hay, I take the dogs out back and sit down at the patio table. A few minutes later, Damien heads over.

"No Lexi?"

"She ran down to Hannah's shop to grab some stuff for Dave and Maggie."

"Cool. Mel's down at the kitchen interviewing for our new kitchen staff. Eden's helping her since she knows what to look for."

"Lexi and I are so happy for her. For both of you. We can see a real difference now that she's not dealing with Daniel."

"Yeah. I finally feel like I have my woman back. Listen, can I tell you a secret? And before I do, you will need to promise not to tell Lexi, so I wanna give you the chance to say no."

"As long as it's not something that will bite me in the ass, I'll do it."

I smile. "I went jewelry shopping this morning."

"A ring?"

"Yeah."

"Dude, that's amazing. Congratulations." Damien extends his hand.

I accept his handshake. "Thanks, man."

"Any thoughts on how?"

I shake my head. "No, but just something simple and private."

He nods. "I don't think Mel would like a big public display."

"I don't either. I'm thinking I might do it right here in the garden."

"Let me know if you decide what night. That way, I can keep Lexi away." Damien laughs.

I laugh with him and say, "Oh, you don't need to do that."

"Trust me, I do. She loves you two, and she'll be so excited that she might interrupt."

"Got it." I nod.

"She can be a handful!" Damien laughs.

I can't help but laugh, too. "Oh, Mel has her moments, too."

"I can only imagine." He rolls his eyes.

"Hey, just realized I'm being rude. How about a beer?"

"Sounds good."

"Be right back." I grab a couple of beers and head back outside.

"Here's to you and Mel taking the next step."

"Here, here."

"What do you think Daniel's problem was with Mel?"

I shrug my shoulders. "I'm not sure, but I get a feeling he's up to something he shouldn't be, and Mel would never have let him get away with it. She's good at her job, and if he was doing anything illegal, she'd find it."

"That makes sense. Or he was pissed that he couldn't have her."

"That also makes sense. I mean, I would hate not being with her."

"Yeah. I'd be lost without Lexi." Just as Damien says that, we hear her car pull into the driveway. Moments later, Lexi walks over to the fence.

"Hate to interrupt bro-time, but I need a hand with the food bags. Mikael loaded them for me."

"Be right there," Damien says.

"I'm cool if you finish your beer first. I can bring the other stuff in."

"Thanks, babe." Damien smiles at his wife. Damien finishes his beer and gets up. "Ah, the life of a husband," he jokes.

I watch Damien head home to help Lexi. All I can think about is how much I want that life. And I don't want to wait. I quickly formulate a plan and head into the kitchen to see if I need anything. I grab my phone and text Damien.

J: Tonight's the night

D: Where?

J: The garden

D: Good luck! I'll take Lexi to dinner/movie

J: Thanks

I run out to the store to grab a couple of things I'm missing for dinner. I also stop and grab a bottle of champagne.

When I get home, I prep dinner and put the champagne in the fridge to chill. I lay a dress out on the bed for her along with a hand-written note.

Requesting the honor of your presence in the garden for dinner.

Mel gets home a little after four.

"So, how did it go?" I ask, barely able to contain my excitement.

"Thanks to Eden, I was able to hire the entire staff we'll need. I have all their information, so we just need to decide when we want them to start."

"How about we work on all that tomorrow?"

"Sounds good. I'm gonna go shower and change before dinner, if that's cool."

"Of course, love."

While Mel's showering, I get the table set up outside. I'm just putting the plates out when she comes out. My mouth waters when I see her barefoot in the yellow sundress I laid out.

"You're stunning," I say, looking her up and down.

"You look pretty damn incredible yourself." I'm wearing cream-colored cotton pants and a blue button down shirt. Inside my pants pocket is a small box that's going to change our lives forever. I ignore the butterflies in my stomach as I escort my woman out to the garden.

"Dinner smells delicious," she says. "And the table's beautiful."

"Thank you." A light blue tablecloth covers the table. A vase of daisies is flanked on each side by white tapers. The flames dance in the light breeze. A mix of eighties love songs softly plays as we dine. My stomach's in knots as I work up the courage to ask my woman easily the most important question ever.

The scent of garlic fills the air. I pour two glasses of Moscato. "To us." We clink glasses and each take a sip before we dig into our garlic shrimp scampi with linguine. After we finish eating, I know it's now or never, so I take a couple of deep breaths, my hand in my pocket touching the box.

I stand and walk so I'm facing Mel's chair. She turns to look at me.

"Baby, I love you so much, and I'm so grateful to be on this journey with you. I'm especially excited about our new chapter. I can barely remember my life before you were in it, and I never want to experience that again."

I take the ring box out of my pocket and get down on one knee. I look at Mel's face and see tears forming in her beautiful eyes. I open the box, and when she sees the ring, her face lights up.

"Melissa, my love, will you do me the honor of becoming my wife?"

"Oh my god, yes, Judd. I love you."

I slide the ring onto her finger and pull her up into my arms. Her lips meet mine as I twirl her around. This is, by far, the happiest moment I've ever experienced, and it's all thanks to the beautiful woman in my arms. I put her on her feet, but keep my arms around her. We move together to the music, completely lost in each other.

"There aren't enough words to tell you how happy I am right now."

"No words needed. I can tell, my love." I smile at my love.

"The ring is stunning. I love that it's a butterfly." She holds her hand in front of her face and gazes at the ring.

"The minute I saw it, I knew it was the one." I take her hand and look down at the ring. It looks so good on her beautiful finger.

"How long have you been planning this?"

"I've been thinking about it for a while, but I just bought the ring this morning. Damien's the only one who knows. He took Lexi out to dinner and a movie so she wouldn't see us out here. He was afraid she'd get so excited, she'd interrupt."

Mel laughs. "Yeah, she probably would. You have no idea how badly she wanted us to get together."

"Damien mentioned it. He told me he had to keep on her to not push too hard."

"That sounds like Lexi. I love her to death, but sometimes, she doesn't know when to back off. But I wouldn't change a single thing about her."

"Yeah."

"I definitely want to tell her, but not tonight. Tonight, I just wanna be alone with you."

"And how might you wish to celebrate?" I drawl with a cocky grin.

"Oh, I think you know! Oh, and by the way, I'm completely commando under this dress."

I scoop my beautiful fiancée up in my arms and carry her right to our bedroom. We don't emerge again until morning.

Chapter Twenty

Mel

After some much-needed sleep, Judd and I are enjoying a light brunch out in the garden when we see Damien and Lexi. Keeping my hand hidden behind me, I walk over to the fence. Damien winks at me then heads over to talk to Judd.

"Do you have a few minutes to chat?" I ask Lexi.

"For you, of course. Come on over."

I head through the gate and follow Lexi to her patio.

"Can I get you something to drink?" Lexi asks.

"Thanks, but I'm good."

"Okay. What did you want to talk about?"

"I have some big news."

"Bigger than retiring?"

"Yeah." I hold out my hand, and Lexi screams so loud, Damien and Judd look over, then start laughing. Damien climbs over the fence, and he and Judd go sit in the garden.

"Oh my god, girl! When?"

"Last night."

"Congratulations! I couldn't be happier for you!" She jumps up and squalls. She grabs me, hugs me, and we bounce together, both of us grinning.

"Thank you. I couldn't be happier!" We sit back down. "There's something else, though."

She tilts her "What?"

I take her hands in mine. "Will you be my matron of honor?"

Lexi's opens her mouth wide. "Are you kidding? Of course I will!" Tears stream down her face.

"I'm so glad. I want to ask Tammy and Allie to be bridesmaids, if that's okay with you."

"Honey, it's your wedding, so it's whatever you want."

"Thank you. We haven't talked dates yet, so I'll have to let you know."

"You mean you didn't do that last night? What were you doing then?" she teases.

"If I have to tell you that!" I laugh.

"Oh, I know. Save a horse, ride a cowboy!" She twirls an invisible lasso.

I slap my hand over my mouth. "Oh my god, Lexi!"

"Oh, don't you dare deny it. I know you've taken plenty of rides on that gorgeous man." She smirks.

"Well, yeah, I have, and damn, he's fuckin' incredible." I wave my hands in front of me.

Lexi jumps up and gives me a big hug. "This is so amazing. We need to have an engagement party."

I swat my hand toward her. "Oh, please don't go to any trouble for me."

Lexi puts a finger over my lips. "Hush, you. I'll give you the details when I have them. My first official duty as matron of honor."

Once Lexi gets something in her head, there's no changing her mind, so I sigh. "Okay, thank you so much."

"Yay! How about we go join the boys?"

"Yeah, let's go." We jump up and, holding hands, we skip over to the guys.

"My lord, woman. We heard you all the way over here," Damien teases Lexi.

"I couldn't help it. I'm so happy!" Lexi clamps her hand on Judd's shoulder. "Thank you for making my girl the happiest woman ever."

"My pleasure, ma'am." Judd tips his cowboy hat toward Lexi.

"And she asked me to be her matron of honor," Lexi says, grinning from ear to ear.

"That's perfect, since Judd asked me to be his best man," Damien says.

"Yay! That means you get to help me plan the engagement party. Mel already agreed to let me do it."

"Why do I suspect she didn't have a choice?" Damien teases.

Lexi's hands fly to her hips. "What are you tryin' to say, husband?"

"Um, nothing," Damien says, still smiling.

"That's what I thought," Lexi says with a wink, and we all laugh. "Come on, Damien. We need to get home and get plans made."

"So, I guess I'm going," Damien shrugs his shoulders as he gets up, still smiling.

Judd and I sit on the bench laughing as we watch Lexi nearly pull Damien's arm out of its socket.

"You're gonna have your hands full with her as matron of honor."

"She means well. I can handle her."

"Who else were you thinking of asking to be bridesmaids?"

"Allie and Tammy. I love the other girls, but they are more Lexi's friends than mine."

"Makes sense. I'm gonna ask Dane and Jay."

"Thank you so much for wanting to include Jay."

"Of course. I know he's like a brother to you, so he should be included."

"You never stop amazing me."

"And I never will."

"I know we're going to get pressured to pick a date, but I definitely want to get some time on our new venture under our belt first."

"I agree. I think we should wait until after the farmer's market closes. I don't want you taking on too much."

"Right. But please know, if you wanted to, I'd marry you right now."

"I know, sweetie. But we would need to get our license first."

"Yeah, and I know we need a date set before we do that."

"How does it work in Pennsylvania? I never had any reason to check."

"We just need to go to the courthouse and apply. At least, that's how it was when I, well, you know."

"I do. We can look it up to make sure."

"Yeah. But right now, I want to reach out to our new employees as I'd like them to start Monday, if they're available."

"Okay. I can help you make calls."

"That would be great."

After we get commitments from all the workers that they'll be there Monday, we make final plans.

"I can't believe this is really happening. I've had so many dreams come true since I met you," I say.

"You're my dream come true, baby. I can't wait until I can call you Mrs. Walker."

"Me too. Let's pick a date."

"I was hoping you'd say that."

"What do you think about mid-October?"

"I had a slightly different date in mind."

"Oh yeah? What?"

"Halloween."

"Oh, that's perfect. Would you be opposed to a Halloween-themed wedding?"

"If that's what you want, I'm in. I want this to be a day you'll never forget."

"No, this needs to be what we want. I'm not getting married. We are."

"But I always thought it was the bride's day." Judd turns his palms upwards.

"Maybe some people feel that way, but not me. This is our day." I wave my hand pointing at each of us.

"Well, I love the idea of the theme. That day is so important to me."
Judd puts his hand over his chest.

"Oh yeah? Why?" I stick my tongue out.

"Woman! I know you can't have forgotten." He wraps his arm
around my waist.

"No way I could ever forget the first time I was naked with you!" I
grab his ass and squeeze hard.

"I'll also never forget that costume. Any chance that could be your
wedding dress?"

"Judd! Honestly! I cannot get married in a low-cut black lace dress
with knee high black boots." I shake my head side to side.

"What? It's so damn sexy." He pulls me tight against him.

"Tell you what. Let me pick something a little more modest, and I'll
wear the black dress on our honeymoon."

"Deal." Judd kisses the top of my head.

"I need to go make a couple of calls before Lexi spoils my news."

Judd laughs. "Allie and Tammy?"

"Yeah."

"I'm gonna take the girls outside while you call them." Judd calls
Daisy and Lily and the three of them walk out to the back yard.

"I'll join you when I'm done."

After Allie and Tammy squeal and agree to be bridesmaids, I walk
out back. Judd's sitting in the grass playing with the girls, so I join them.
I lie back and start gazing at the clouds. Judd joins me, and as we're
laying there, some light rain starts falling.

"You wanna go in?" Judd asks.

"Nah. A little rain won't hurt."

"But your hair." Judd smirks.

"When have I ever been *that* girl?" I throw my hands in the air.

"Point taken." He laughs.

"Truth is, I've always wanted to dance in the rain, but never had
anyone to do it with."

I watch Judd get up. He holds out his hands and helps me up. "Wait
right here." Judd turns on the outside stereo and *Boogie* plays. Judd
grabs my hand and tries to get me to dance.

"I can't. Someone might see."

"We're the only ones out here." Just as he finishes saying that, the rain picks up, and we're drenched. "Come on, baby."

"Oh, what the hell." I take Judd's hand and start moving my hips. We're disco-dancing around the yard completely rain-soaked while the dogs lay under the patio roof. I can only imagine what they're thinking as they watch us. We're laughing so hard, we never notice our neighbors walk out onto their patio.

"What on Earth?" Lexi yells over.

"Mel said she always wanted to dance in the rain!" Judd calls back.

"You two are crazy," Lexi says. She doubles over.

"I think it looks fun," Damien says and runs out from under his patio. He joins us dancing and motions for Lexi.

"No way in hell," Lexi says, her arms crossed in front of her.

"Sorry, babe, but you're doin' this," Damien says. He runs back, puts Lexi over his shoulder, and carries her out into the yard. She tries to give him a scowl, but she quickly joins in, and four adults are now dancing in the pouring rain. And, miraculously enough, no alcohol was involved.

When the song ends, we're all standing there laughing. "I need to point out that every single dog is sitting there dry while us dinguses are soaked," I say.

"Yeah, but we're having fun," Lexi says.

"And you didn't wanna do it," Damien teases.

Lexi sticks her tongue out at Damien and takes off. He chases her, and again, she's over his shoulder. He waves to us and carries her inside. "Hmmm, wonder what they're off to do," I joke.

Judd laughs. "Are you ready to go in?" Judd asks.

"Nah. I wanna dance some more."

By the time we're done, our clothes weigh a ton from all the water. We strip down to our underwear on the back patio and wring out our clothes. I take the wet clothes and put them in the washer. Once we're out of our underwear and showered, we start the washer and sit down to watch some TV.

"Thank you for the dance," I say as I rest my head on Judd's broad shoulder.

"My pleasure, ma'am."

The next thing I know, it's morning, and I'm lying in bed. I look over and Judd's laying there watching me. "I don't remember going to bed," I say.

"You fell asleep on my shoulder, so I carried you in here."

"My knight in shining armor."

"Anything for my queen." He pulls me in close and kisses me. "How about we treat ourselves to breakfast out this morning?"

"I'd love to. How about we go to Eden's restaurant? She allows dogs at the outside tables."

"Great. Then maybe we'll stop at the dog park."

"The magical dog park. You know, someone should write books about our dog park." I smile.

"What kinda books?"

"A fun rom-com where all the couples meet like Damien and Lexi did."

Judd laughs. "I'd read that."

"It would be especially fun if the books were written, at least partially, from the dog's POV."

"Could you imagine if Dave talked?" Judd and I laugh together.

"If he did, I picture him being a total smartass."

"Oh, most definitely." Judd nods his head up and down.

I pack a bag with some tennis balls, a collapsible water bowl, and a couple of bottles of water. Judd takes the dogs outside and gets them into the truck. I finish packing the bag and join him. The dogs lay down on the backseat while we drive to the diner.

We get to Garden of Eden and take a seat at one of the empty outdoor tables. After last night's rain, all the clouds have moved out, and the sky boasts a majestic bright blue. The sun is shining, and we have another day of comfortable mid-seventy temperatures.

Judd goes in to order while I get the girls set under the table. He returns with two huge cups of iced coffee. He sets mine in front of me, and the delicious scent of hazelnut fills my nose.

"Yum! My favorite," I say.

"I could say the same about you."

"And now I need to vomit." We look up, and Abby's standing there scowling.

"Leave us the fuck alone," Judd warns.

"This is a public place," Abby says.

"But it's part of my restaurant, and I reserve the right to ask anyone to leave." I turn and see Eden standing there with our breakfast. "Please leave, or I'll be forced to call the police." Abby turns on her heel with a glare and storms off. After placing our plates down on the table, Eden says, "What was that about, if I may ask?"

I look at Judd, who responds, "It's fine. She's my ex from before I moved here."

"And let me guess. She wants you back."

"So she says, but she ain't getting me. I belong to this beauty. The proof is on her finger."

Eden grabs Mel's hand and squeals. "Oh my god, congratulations, you two! Such a beautiful ring!"

"Thank you."

"What are we celebrating out here?" Johnny asks when he joins us.

"These two kids are tying the knot," Eden says.

"Nice! Blessings to you both," Johnny says, shaking Judd's hand.

"Thank you," I say.

"Have you picked a date?" Eden asks.

"Yeah, but I haven't told Lexi yet, so if she's not the first one to know the date, I could be in trouble."

Eden laughs, but she nods, knowing Lexi will kick my butt if I tell anyone else first. Eden and Johnny head back inside after giving the girls some head pats.

After we finish breakfast, Judd takes our dishes inside and pays the check. When we pull into the dog park lot, we see Alex and Dean and their dog, Holly. Before we get our arms ripped off, we let Daisy and Lily off leash, and they run over to where Holly's laying.

Judd throws a few tennis balls to the girls, and all three of them get a case of the zoomies. We all laugh as they race around the park.

"It looks like NASCAR but with dogs," I joke as Judd and I sit on the empty bench next to Alex and Dean.

"I'm glad you guys came. Holly was bored by herself, and we were just getting ready to leave," Alex says.

"Maybe she needs a friend," I say.

"Hush," Dean teases. "Actually, we've been talking about it, but Holly's getting a little older."

"Yeah, that makes it tough. Well, you're always welcome for a play-date," I say.

"Thanks, love," Alex says.

"What do ya say we go play with the dogs and let the ladies chat?" Dean asks.

Judd gets up and they stroll out to where the dogs are playing. We watch them for a few minutes.

"I love a man who's kind to animals," Alex says.

"Me too. Those two have Judd wrapped around their paws."

"Oh yeah. I think Dean loves Holly more than he loves me," she jokes, and I laugh. "So, what's new with you? Besides retirement, of course. Lexi told me about your new venture. Yell if you need any help or advice at the market."

"Thanks, and actually there is something even newer."

"Wow, what?"

I hold out my hand, and Alex throws her arms around me. "Con-gratulations, woman. Mmm, spending the rest of your life with that hottie! Not too shabby for Rachel," Alex says, quoting a line from one of our favorite shows, *Friends*.

"No complaints here. I never expected to give my heart to another man, but Judd left me no choice. He's incredible."

"We're all very lucky ladies."

"That we are."

"Wanna have a little fun with the guys?" Alex asks, a gleam in her eyes.

"Of course!"

"Keep glancing their way as we pretend to talk and laugh. It drives Dean crazy."

"Okay, naughty girl."

"Hey, it's worth getting caught!"

"Oh, hell yeah!"

I think about some of my favorite challenges on *Impractical Jokers,* and that makes it easy for me to laugh hysterically. My all-time favorite will always be the triple punishment where Joe picks out tattoos for the other three guys.

We keep glancing out at Dean and Judd, throwing in the occasional point for good measure, and we're definitely driving them crazy. That only makes Alex and I laugh harder, both of us with tears pouring down our faces.

"Uh oh, they're headed our way," I say.

"We're in trouble now!" Alex says.

"And just what are you two troublemakers up to?" Dean asks, arms crossed across his chest.

"Yeah," Judd says.

"Whatever do you mean?" Alex says, batting her eyelashes.

"Uh-uh, woman. That innocent act don't work on me," Dean says.

"But we are innocent," I say.

"My ass," Judd adds.

"Well, I never," Alex says.

"Me either," I add, barely able to keep a straight face.

"I think these two naughty ladies need to be sent straight to bed," Dean says.

"Oh, yes, please," Alex says.

"Mmm, yeah. I agree, cowboy," I say to Judd.

Judd and I load up the dogs and head home. And as soon as we're inside, he sends me right to bed, and if he thought I was naughty at the park, he had a surprise in store in the bedroom!

Chapter Twenty-One

Judd

As summer progresses, our new business venture takes off, due in large part to Mel's hard work. She's in her element, and I love watching her in action.

Most of Mel's free time is being hogged by Lexi. It reminds me of watching Monica plan Phoebe's wedding. All I can do is sit back and laugh while Mel tries not to pull her hair out.

"That's it, I'm firing her!" Mel says after one particularly long planning marathon.

"You can't fire your best friend," I say as calmly as possible.

"I can if I want us to stay friends!"

"She means well. Damien did warn me that it might get like this."

"I know she means well, but good grief! She has me a stressed out mess."

"Well, if you are, it sure looks cute on you."

"Maybe we should elope."

"I would if that's what you really wanted, but you deserve a wedding."

"Awww, you're too sweet."

"Maybe Tammy and Allie can help get her under control."

"They tried."

"Ah."

I hear Mel's cell ringing.

"Lexi?" I ask.

"Mmmm. Hey, Lexi. What's up?" Mel says and walks into the kitchen. She returns a little while later looking completely frazzled. I swear I heard the words you're fired come out of Mel's mouth.

"What happened?"

"I had to remind her that while I appreciate her help, she's the matron of honor, not the wedding planner. She was trying to pick out the menu. I think I got her under control for now."

"Speaking of the menu, who were you thinking of asking to cater?"

"I was going to offer it to my kitchen staff first."

"Exactly what I was thinking."

"The other thing we need to decide is where to have it. I would really love to do it up at the lake house."

"Baby, that would be amazing."

"But, is it fair to ask everyone to travel that far?"

"Hey, it's our wedding. We can have it wherever we want. Besides, I think our friends would be willing."

"Okay, then it's settled. We just need to order invitations."

"How about we do that tomorrow? Then we can stop by and ask the staff if they want to cater."

"Sounds good. And we'll pay for their travel."

"Oh, absolutely. I was figuring we would."

The next morning, we head out to do our errands. The staff agrees to cater our wedding, so that's one less thing for Mel to worry about. We're just getting home when Mel's cell rings.

"I have to head down to the market," she says when she disconnects.

"What's going on?"

"Katie's not feeling well, so I'm gonna go cover the stall for the rest of the day."

I got the impression when Mel hired her she wasn't keen on working, but I kept my opinion to myself.

"Okay. You want me to go with you?"

"I'm good, but thanks for the offer."

After Mel heads out, I sit on the couch, and no sooner do I plop down, my landline rings. I look down and see a number I don't recognize.

"Hello."

"Hello, Judd."

"Hi, Aunt Mimi."

"Sorry to bother you."

"You're no bother, ma'am."

"You're a sweet man. Is Mel home?"

"No, she had to run down to the farmer's market."

"Would you mind coming over? I need to speak with you about something, and I'd prefer to do it without my Melissa."

I raise an eyebrow. "Um, okay. What's your address?" I write her address down and say, "I'll be there shortly."

I get in my truck and drive in silence, trying to figure out what news is waiting for me. I park in Aunt Mimi's driveway. She must have heard my truck. The door opens just as I'm about to knock.

She greets me with a big hug then guides me into her dining room where I see a man about my age. He's dressed in a three-piece suit, but it's the serious look on his face that has me worried.

"Have a seat," she says. "This is my attorney, David Crenshaw."

"A pleasure, Mr. Walker," David says, extending his hand. I return the gesture then take a seat.

"I know you and my niece noticed my coughing at the birthday party," Aunt Mimi says. I nod. "I wasn't exactly honest with her. I have lung cancer, and I'm terminal."

"Oh, I'm so sorry." I feel like I just got punched in the heart.

"No. Stop that now. I'm not looking for pity. It's why I didn't tell my Melissa. But I want to make sure all of my affairs are in order. I'm planning to leave everything to Melissa, but I need help to hopefully prevent her any undue stress."

I gently cover her hand with mine. "What can I do?"

Aunt Mimi presses her lips together. "Agree to be my executor."

I furrow my brows. "Why me? Why not Mel?"

"Easy. Her mom and her sister. I fear they'll fight her every step of the way. But if I put you in charge, that will take the pressure off of her. I know it may seem unfair to put you in the middle."

I lean in toward Aunt Mimi. "Don't give that a second thought. I know why you're doing this, and honestly, I agree. I've seen how they treat Mel, and I've seen how she feels about you. She's going to be devastated, so I will honor your wish."

Aunt Mimi smiles weakly. "I know they can still contest, and I can't prevent that, but this way, they are fighting you and not Mel."

"Absolutely. What do I need to do?"

"I have some documents for you to sign," David says, opening his briefcase. He runs through everything with me, and I sign where needed. "I'll have a copy at my office, and Mimi will have one here. Would you like one as well?"

"No," Aunt Mimi says before I have a chance to respond. I look at her slightly confused, but I'm sure she has a reason. "I have one more favor to ask."

"And that is?" I ask hesitantly..

"Please don't tell Melissa I'm sick."

I shake my head slowly. "I can't keep that from her."

"Please, Judd. I know what a difficult position that puts you in. But you know as well as I do that if Mel finds out, she'd put her life on hold to care for me. And I don't want her doin' that. Especially now that you two are getting married."

"But Aunt Mimi." I wring my hands.

"No. I'm adamant about this, and you know I'm a tough old broad."

"Okay," I say with a sigh. I don't feel good about this, but how can I not honor her wish at a time like this?

"You're a good man, Judd Walker. And I'm counting on you to be there for my niece. She's going to need you more than ever when I'm gone."

"I love you," I say, fighting back tears.

"None of that. Mel can't see you upset." She holds my hand.

I nod. "I know. I'll have it together before she gets home."

"Thank you. Most of all for finally treating my sweet Melissa the way she should be treated." She smiles at me.

I tip my hat at her. "My pleasure, ma'am."

"Hers, too, I'm sure." Aunt Mimi winks at me.

"Aunt Mimi!" I exclaim with a grin. She laughs while David tries to stifle a laugh of his own.

"Do you need anything else from me?" David asks Aunt Mimi.

"No. Thank you."

I give Aunt Mimi a gentle hug, then David and I walk out together.

"Thank you for doing this for her."

"I'm still not sure not telling her niece is the right thing, but I will honor her request."

"I tried to talk her into telling Melissa, but she's stubborn."

"Yeah."

"Listen, if you need anything, please call my office," he says, handing me a card.

"Will do." I sit in my truck for a few minutes trying to process everything that just happened. But how can I?

I start my truck and drive towards home, but instead of pulling into my driveway, I pull into Damien's. He opens the door when I knock.

"Hey man, what's up?" Damien asks.

"Lexi here?"

"No. Cassie needed her at the club. Why?"

"I need to talk to you, but before I do, it's something you can't tell Lexi. So, please tell me no if you would prefer not to keep anything from her."

"Does it concern her?"

"No, of course not."

"Then, let's go sit out back. You look like you need a friend."

Damien stops in the kitchen and grabs a couple beers. He hands me one, and we go sit on the back patio.

"What happened?" Damien asks when we sit down.

"I just left Aunt Mimi's house."

"Without Mel?" he asks a little bit surprised.

"Yeah. She called me and asked me to come over. So, you remember when we went to Mel's mom's house for her stepfather's birthday?"

"Yeah."

"Well, Aunt Mimi had a couple bad coughing fits, but she played them off. Mel was worried, and it turns out she was right."

"Oh no. What's wrong?"

"Terminal cancer."

His face scrunches slightly. "But why did she have you come over? Just to tell you?"

"She's leaving everything to Mel, but she's worried that her Mom or Trish will give Mel a hard time if she's executress. So, she asked me to be executor so that if they do try to fight, it won't be on Mel."

"Oh, man. I'm sorry. How are you gonna tell Mel?"

"That's part of the problem. Aunt Mimi asked me not to tell her. She doesn't want Mel to drop everything and take care of her."

"What did you say?"

"I agreed. Reluctantly. Dude, how can I not tell her? But how can I go against her aunt's wishes?"

"I wish there was an easy answer."

"Me too. And even if I don't tell her, how am I going to hide that something's wrong?"

He shrugs as he takes a drink. "I wish I could be more help, man."

"I know." I sigh. "I'll figure it out. Thanks for listening."

"Anytime."

"I better head home and get myself composed before Mel gets home."

"Good luck. I'm always here."

"Thanks."

When I get home, I sit down on the couch, and both dogs come over, each laying a head on one of my legs.

"Thanks, girls," I say, patting each of them on the head. "What am I gonna do about your momma?" Two pairs of brown eyes look up at me.

I'm in the kitchen getting dinner ready when Mel comes in.

"Mmm, something smells delicious. And the food does, too."

"Cute."

"Thanks. Hope you had an uneventful day."

"Yep," I lie. "How was yours?"

"Great! We completely sold out of everything. I'm so grateful to have such a great kitchen staff. I'll have to stop and stock up on the way to the market in the morning."

"Not expecting Katie?"

"Honestly, I don't ever expect her back. She didn't seem too keen on the job. But it's all good. I can handle it until I find someone else."

"How about we both work there tomorrow?"

"If you're sure, but don't you have stuff to do here?"

"Nothing that can't wait. I wanna do this."

"Then, it's settled. It'll be fun to work together."

"Yeah, then we can come home and play together."

"Mmm. I like the way you think, my sexy cowboy."

"How about after dinner, we hit the hot tub?"

"That sounds perfect. I could use a good soak."

"Why don't you have a seat? Dinner is almost ready."

"Thank you."

A few minutes later, I put a plate in front of Mel, and her eyes go wide. There's nothing I love more than taking care of this amazing woman.

"I can't believe I'm staring at a plate of sautéed shrimp, risotto, and asparagus. Everything smells divine, and I can't wait to dig in," Mel says. I bring a bottle of Moscato and two glasses to the table and sit down across from my fiancée.

She tries a bite of everything, and exclaims, "Oh my god, Judd, everything is so good. Thank you."

"My pleasure, love."

After we finish eating, which she did in record speed, we clean up then get changed into swimwear. She climbs into the hot tub while I turn the jets on, then join her. I put my arm around her and pull her close. She rests her head on my shoulder.

Moments like these are my favorite. I don't need fancy trips or expensive stuff. I would much rather just spend time with Mel and the dogs. After a couple very relaxing hours, I start feeling sleepy, and I let out a loud yawn.

"I think I need to get to bed," I say. "I'm exhausted."

"I am, too, baby. Let's go."

I get out and hold out my hand to help Mel climb out. I wrap her in a towel and hold her tight against me. There's something so calming about having this woman in my arms.

We call the dogs inside, and I lock up while Mel's getting ready for bed. By the time I get in bed, she's already sound asleep.

Of course, sleep eludes me. All I can think about is Aunt Mimi. I finally drift off, but to say that it was a restless night is an under-statement.

She's up and gone before I get up, so I get dressed, grab a quick bite to eat, and head down to the market.

Chapter Twenty-Two

Mel

After an early morning rush, I get a short lull in customers. I look up and see Judd heading my way.

"Well, well. Hey, sleepyhead," I tease.

"You should have woken me."

"You looked so peaceful. I didn't have the heart."

"I'm here now. Put me to work."

"I need to restock. I had quite a rush this morning, and it should pick up again in about an hour."

Judd follows me to the walk-in freezer at the back of our stall, and we carry more meals out, putting them in our display case. We're just finishing up when we see Jay headed our way.

"Long way to go for a lunch run," Judd says.

"Yeah. Wonder what's up," I say.

"Hey, lovebirds," Jay says when he reaches our stall.

"What are you doing here in the middle of the day?" I ask. "I mean, always glad to see my friend, but curious."

"Well, let's just say a little birdie had a chat with me. I'm guessing you know what she told me."

"He was after you, too?" I ask.

"Allie didn't give me specifics, just that she heard some rumblings, and that it would be in my best interest to retire."

"She told me that she heard Daniel was desperate to get rid of me. Nothing more specific."

"I'd love to know what the hell is going on," Jay says.

"Me too," I say. "What are you gonna do now?"

"Nothing for a bit. I need some time to process. I have enough money put away that I can take some time."

"Hey, that gives you more time to woo Tammy."

"Yeah. Except, so far, she hasn't shown a bit of interest."

"That's not the impression I got from her. I think she likes you."

"Well, she hasn't given me any indication."

"Be patient. I also got the feeling she's been through a lot. If there's one thing I know about, it's protecting my heart."

"And look at us now," Judd adds. "You'll get there. If not with Tammy, then with someone."

"Thanks, guys. So, what's good today?"

"Everything. We have an amazing kitchen staff."

"Okay. I'll take a lasagna meal, and a shrimp scampi meal."

"They're on the house, my friend."

"No way. I'm paying. This is your business."

"Fine, then you get the friends and family discount. Ten percent off."

"Thanks, girl. Hey, I gotta say, retirement really suits you. I can see how much more relaxed you are."

"Thanks to this guy."

"I wonder how much Mr. O'Laughlin knows about what Daniel's up to," Jay says.

"I'm guessing very little. He would never have stood for the way I was treated."

"Pretty much what I was thinking. From day one, he never treated the women any differently. Way ahead of his time."

"It's why I stayed so long. I never felt like I had to work harder than my male counterparts to prove my worth."

"It actually makes me sad that Daniel's taking everything he built and treating it like his little playground."

"Great analogy, given he acts like a petulant child most of the time."

"Glad neither of us have to worry. I just hope Allie doesn't get caught up in anything."

"Same, especially after the way she helped us."

"Well, you know, if something happens, we could always hire her to handle HR stuff for us," Judd adds.

"Which I would in a heartbeat. I know how good she is."

"Well, I gotta be on my way. I'm gonna take these meals to Full Moon and see if Tammy will at least have dinner with me, even if just as friends."

"Have fun," I say with a wink.

Jay waves as he walks away. No sooner is he gone but a new rush starts, and Judd and I barely get a chance to talk for the rest of the day.

I feel like something's off with him, but I can't put my finger on it. I hope I didn't do or say something to upset him. But for now, I need to put that out of my head and just focus on our customers. I make a mental note to talk to him when we get home.

By the end of the day, we had to restock several times, and we did great. I thought it would take us time to build a following, but things have taken off like wildfire. I may need to hire more cooks at the rate we're selling out.

We get home and Judd plops down on the couch. "How about we give ourselves a break and order delivery?" Judd rumbles.

"I could go for Chinese unless you were hungry for something else."

"Oh, I intend to satisfy *that* hunger later. For now, Chinese sounds great."

I order the food then join Judd on the couch.

"Hey, babe, are you okay?" I ask.

"Yeah, why?"

"It just feels like something's off. Like you have something on your mind. You know you can talk to me."

"I know that, sweetheart, and I promise I would talk to you if I needed to. I promise I'm fine."

"Are you sure?"

"Yeah. Nothin' to worry about darlin'. I swear."

"Okay," I say, but I'm not convinced. Not wanting to push too hard, I let it go, at least for now.

While we wait for dinner, Judd goes through the mail. He hands me a fancy-looking envelope.

"Wow," I say after I open it.

"What's that?"

"We're invited to the yearly O'Laughlin retirement ball."

"You wanna go?"

"If you do."

"It would be my honor to escort my lady to the ball."

"Then I'll RSVP."

"Great. Hey, maybe you and Lexi could go shopping."

"Ugh. I hate clothes shopping."

"Words I never thought I'd hear come out of a woman's mouth."

"Just was never for me. Now, if it was shopping at a record store, I could stay there for days. But clothes, nah. If not for working at O'Laughlin, I'd have nothing but jeans and tees."

"What do you think I should wear?"

"I hate to say, but it's black tie, so you'll need to rent a tux."

"Totally fine. I'll be your penguin, my love."

I giggle. "You're just the cutest," I say.

"I'll hit the rental place in the morning, then meet you at the market, unless you need me there since it gets busy early."

"I'll be fine."

"Cool. Anything special you wanna watch while we eat?"

"Actually, yeah. I'm in the mood for comedy, so how about we re-watch *Brooklyn Nine-Nine*?"

"I never saw it."

I stare at him with my mouth wide open. "What? Not even one episode? Oh, you poor, poor man. Get ready to laugh your ass off."

Imitating me, he bounces and claps his hands. "Can't wait." That earns him a raspberry. He laughs and I swat him with a pillow.

I feed the dogs while we wait. Once the food comes, I make up two plates while Judd sets up TV tables. I grab him a beer and a wine cooler for myself. We end up watching the entire first season of the show.

"*Nine-Nine!*" Judd exclaims.

With my best evil laugh, I say, "I've converted another one!"

"I can't believe I never saw this. I love the heist."

"Just wait. There's plenty more of them."

Judd raises his arms above his head. "Well, I'm hooked."

"Yay! I just love Rosa. She's such a badass!"

"Judd likes Terry." I laugh at his impression of Terry always speaking in third person.

"The whole cast is really great. They all just fit so well together."

"I can't wait to watch more seasons."

I'm about to answer when I hear whimpering. I look over, and both girls are standing at the back door. "I think some ladies need to take care of business," I say, laughing.

I open the door, and the girls take off to their favorite part of the yard to potty. Judd and I walk out and sit in the garden. I grab a couple of tennis balls out of the toy bin and throw them. That's all it takes for a round of zoomies. I could sit and watch these two play all day.

"I'm so glad you found those gorgeous angels," Judd says.

"Me too. I shudder to think what may have happened if we hadn't. I can't fathom what would make anyone put puppies in a trash bag and dump them anywhere."

Judd lowers his eyes and shakes his head back and forth. "Yeah." He rubs my back. "But, thanks to the sweetest woman I've ever known, they have a place to call home."

I smile at his kind words. "And I finally get to be a momma."

"An amazing one at that." Judd runs his index finger lightly down my cheek.

I lock eyes with him. "I love you."

"I love you." He pulls me into him.

The girls are finally worn out, so they come over and sit in front of us. "Do you ladies wanna go back in?" I ask. They both run over to the door.

"Smart. Just like their momma," Judd says. "Oh, by the way, I have a surprise for you in the freezer."

"Oooh, what?"

"Go take a look."

I run into the kitchen and open the freezer. "Oh my god! Otter Pops!" I exclaim. "Where did you find those?"

"I remembered you mentioning them once, so I checked online and ordered a couple of boxes."

"How is it possible that you keep getting sweeter?"

"Because of my sweet woman. Oh, and that's not all. I have another surprise."

"You spoil me too much."

"I could never spoil you enough. This is something else I found online."

Judd hands me a plastic tote. I squeal when I see what's inside. Tears fill my eyes. "I can't believe you found these." I just sit and stare at a complete set of vintage Sesame Street Christmas tree ornaments. "How did you know I had these as a child?"

Judd lifts his eyes to the ceiling. "A little birdy may have told me."

Smiling, I say, "I don't know what to say except thank you so much. They were my favorite ornaments."

"You're welcome. And just think. This year, when we decorate our tree, we'll be husband and wife."

"I can't wait to be Mrs. Walker."

"Mmm, I like the way that sounds. Melissa Walker, my incredible wife."

"I think we should start rehearsing for the wedding."

"Oh? Already? What do you want to rehearse?"

"The wedding night."

He scoops me up with a sexy smirk and not another word. He deposits me on the bed and flashes me a look. My clothes fly off.

The next morning, I wake up, still naked, my big sexy man holding me close. After a quick breakfast, I get ready to head down to the farmer's market.

"I'll see you there as soon as I'm done with my fitting," Judd says.

"Sounds great. Love you."

"Love you more."

I'm partway through setting up when I hear a familiar voice. "Hey Jay, what's going on?"

"I'm bored, so thought I'd come hang out. Where's Judd?"

"Getting fitted for a tux."

"For the wedding?"

"No, for the retirement ball."

"Oh, yeah. I got that invite, too. I wasn't gonna go."

"Why not?"

"I dunno."

"You should go. Ask Tammy to be your date."

"Since you're going, okay."

"Cool, cool, cool."

"Been binging *Nine-Nine* again?"

"Yeah. Judd had never seen it, but he's hooked now."

"Noice. Anything I can do to help until Judd gets here?"

"If you could help me serve customers, that would be great. I was swamped yesterday."

"You got it."

By the time Judd arrives, we've already restocked the case four times. I'm lucky Jay stopped by. I really needed the help.

"Hey, guys," Judd says when he arrives. "Thanks for helping my girl out this morning."

"Happy to help. You might need to expand your stall," Jay says.

"I was actually thinking of talking to Art and see if there's something bigger," Judd says.

"Or should we think about getting a store instead of selling here?" I ask.

"I was thinking about that, but it seems like most of our sales come from the busloads that visit the market," Judd says.

"Yeah, that's true. I'd hate to lose those customers. But, a bigger stall would help. If we could get a couple more display cases, we wouldn't have to restock as often," I say.

"If Jay can stay a little while longer, I'll see if I can get a minute with Art now," Judd says.

"Of course," Jay says.

I watch the sexy ass of my cowboy walk away, but I don't get much of a chance to admire him. Another busload arrives, and a line quickly forms at our stall. Jay and I go nuts filling orders. We get a small lull and grab some water.

"Damn, girl. I'm so proud of you. This is amazing."

"Thanks. Have you given any thought to doing something like this? I mean, not exactly this."

"There's a couple of things I've always wanted to try."

"Oh yeah? What?"

"Well, I'd love to own a bar, and I'd love to perform."

"Perform? Like a stripper?"

Jay laughs. "No, silly. Sing and play guitar."

My mouth drops. "Have you been holding out on me? You sing and play? I mean I've heard you at karaoke, but I didn't know it was anything more than that."

"I play at a club a couple nights a week."

"Holy shit. Master secret keeper. I had no idea. I'd love to see you play sometime."

"I don't know. What if you think I'm terrible?" Jay stuffs his hands into his pockets and looks at the floor.

I grab his arm and give him a light squeeze. "Oh, stop it! There's no way you could be terrible. And I bet the women go crazy when you hit the stage."

"Well, I did get my first pair of panties the other night." I snort-laugh, picturing a pair of granny panties smacking his face.

"Oh my god, dude! Oh, shit, here comes another busload. I need to restock."

"I'll do that while you start taking orders."

"Thanks!"

We get this load done and sit down at the small café table Judd found for our stall. I look up and see Judd coming back.

"He is a lifesaver," I say when I see Judd carrying a tray with three burgers and three orders of fries.

"That he is. I'm starving, especially after selling all this delicious-looking food."

"Lunch is served," Judd says as he sets the tray down. "And I have some good news."

"You talked to Art?"

"Yep. And the stall next to us will be vacant in a couple of weeks. He's willing to let us expand as long as we pay the rent for both."

"Absolutely. I can fit at least two more cases, maybe three if we're allowed to take the wall down."

"I asked, and he said yeah. It's not load-bearing, so we're good. The only thing he requested there is that we wait until after the season so the construction isn't going on while customers are here."

"That works. Thank you so much for making that happen."

"Anything for my love."

"I think I just got a cavity," Jay teases.

"Shut it," I say, elbowing him in the side. Hard.

"Ow." Jay rubs his side. Judd and I laugh.

The rest of the day is just as busy as the morning was. Busload after busload of tourists and seniors visit the market today, and even with three of us working, it's still hard keeping up. As much as I love what I'm doing, I'm glad for closing time today.

"Jay, please let me pay you for today," I say.

"No way, girl. I'm happy to help you out."

"Thank you. At least let me give you some food."

"Well, if it's okay, could I take two meals? Tammy enjoyed the food so much, I thought maybe I'd take her food again."

"Of course. It's the least I can do," I say.

"Thanks. I'm gonna head out now. I wanna get cleaned up before I go see Tammy."

"Have fun," I say.

We finish cleaning up after Jay leaves.

"How about leftover Chinese and more *Nine-nine*?" Judd asks.

"Oh lord, I've created a monster."

"Yes you have."

"Well, then, let's go."

We're part way through season two when I hear my cell.

"Hey, Tammy. What's up?"

"I need your help."

"With what?" I ask with a raised eyebrow.

"Jay asked me to go to the ball with him. I don't have a dress, and fashion is not my strong-suit."

"Me either. Wanna go be miserable together tomorrow morning?"

"That would be great."

"We'll find some salesperson to take pity on us. How about I pick you up around nine?"

"Sounds great. Thanks, Mel."

"You bet. See ya in the morning."

After I disconnect, I turn to Judd. "I hate to ask, but would you be okay covering the booth in the morning?"

"Of course. I'll see if Damien wants to help."

"Thanks. I promise Tammy and I will be as quick as possible. Neither of us is thrilled about this whole shopping thing."

"Take your time. You deserve the break."

The next morning, I get to Tammy's a little before nine. She's waiting outside for me and jumps in my car when I pull into her driveway. We head down to our local mall and decide to start at Macy's. We stand in the dress section like two deer caught in headlights when a twenty-something salesperson approaches. I see her name tag says Annabel.

"Can I help you?" Annabel says in a voice far too perky for this time, or any time, of day.

"We both need a formal evening gown," I say.

"Follow me."

Tammy and I trudge behind her. "Do you suddenly feel old?" Tammy whispers.

"Oh yeah," I whisper back.

Annabel looks at each of us for a minute then grabs two dresses, one midnight blue and one emerald green. She hands me the blue dress and gives the green one to Tammy. We each go into a dressing room and try our dress on. I don't know Annabel did it, but she gave me the exact size I needed.

Turning around, I actually like how I look. The top is a bodice with straps. I have just enough breast showing that Judd's gonna be panting. The floor-length bottom flares out at the waist and will hide what I think are problem areas, though Judd never complains.

Tammy's dress is an off the shoulder floor-length gown with a high-leg slit. The color looks stunning against her reddish-brown hair. I'm used to seeing her in jeans and tee-shirts at the bar, so this is quite the change.

"Girl, you look stunning. Jay's gonna be drooling," I say.

"Oh, I think your cowboy's gonna be quite pleased himself."

"We'll take them," I say to Annabel.

After we're back in our clothes, Annabel puts each dress in a garment bag and hands them to us. After we grab matching shoes and evening bags, we head home.

"I feel like Julia Roberts in *Pretty Woman*," Tammy jokes.

"Me too. Hey, since we came this far, how about we pamper ourselves the morning of the ball?"

"How so?"

"Hair, nails, and makeup."

"Oh, why the hell not?"

"Great, do you have a place you like to go?"

"No. One of the girls at work usually cuts my hair, and the rest, I attempt to do myself."

"Okay. I'll book us appointments at the place Lexi booked when she got married."

"Sounds good. I took that Saturday off so I could attend the party."

"Great."

After a few moments of silence, Tammy takes a breath. "Can I ask you something?"

"Sure."

"How come Jay's still single?"

"I'm honestly not sure. When we both started at O'Laughlin fresh out of college, he had a girlfriend. Then one Monday morning, he didn't. When I asked him what happened, he said he didn't wanna talk about it. And that was the last time it was ever mentioned."

"But he would never hurt someone, would he?"

"Absolutely not. I mean, of course, if things didn't work out."

"Oh, I meant like abuse."

"Oh god no. Jay is a sweetheart."

"Sorry. I shouldn't have asked that."

"No, it's okay. You can't be too safe."

"Yeah."

I can't help but wonder if someone hurt Tammy. That would explain why she's so hesitant to get involved with Jay. I hate that this kind of thing still happens, which makes me appreciate a man like Judd even more.

After I drop Tammy off, I head down to see how Judd and Damien are doing at the market. They both look quite frazzled when I arrive, so I jump in and help them, but I can't help but laugh. Two burly men, and this takes them down. I decide to behave and not tease them, especially since they are helping me out, but I'm definitely amused.

"You both did a great job. Thank you," I say.

"How do you do this day in and day out?" Damien asks.

"I don't know. I just do it."

"Well, then you must be Wonder Woman in disguise."

I spin around a few times, and the guys laugh.

"Uh, you can't possibly think you're Wonder Woman."

I turn around, and Abby's standing there. "What can I help *you* with?" I ask, my voice laced with annoyance.

"You can't, but he can," Abby says, pointing at Judd.

"The only thing I can help you do is go the hell back to Texas where you belong," Judd says.

"This is my home now. And you WILL be my man."

"Leave my friends the fuck alone." We all turn and see Lexi standing there, eyes on fire. Abby ducks away from her and takes off.

"Thanks, Lex," I say with a sigh.

"Anytime."

"Now that I'm here, if you want to head out with Lexi, we're good," Judd says to Damien.

"You sure?"

"Yeah," I say. "And please take a couple of meals."

After they pick out a meal each, Damien and Lexi head out.

Judd and I are cleaning up after closing time, and he's especially quiet. When we get home, we grab a quick bite and take the dogs out back. We're sitting in the garden and Judd's still quiet.

"You okay?" I ask.

"Just pissed that you have to keep dealing with those two even after retiring."

"I can handle it."

"Yeah, but you shouldn't have to. And it's all my fault."

Chapter Twenty-Three

Judd

"Why on earth would you think that?" Mel asks.

"I'm the one who brought Abby into your life."

"You did nothing of the sort. She came here on her own. And you certainly had nothing to do with Daniel."

"But it feels like none of this would have happened if not for me."

"That couldn't be further from the truth. I've survived because of you."

Without another word, she grabs my shoulders and crushes her lips to mine. She breaks the kiss as quickly as she started it. "I love you more than life itself. I wouldn't have a life without you. Never forget that."

"I won't. I'm so sorry. It's just having her here."

"I can't imagine how hard it is."

"I just want her to leave us alone."

"Me too, but I promise you, we'll get through this."

"Together."

"Always."

"Thanks, baby."

"You got it, cowboy. Hey, I have an idea. Something we haven't done in a while."

"Oh yeah? What?"

"A ride."

"Babe, you ride me a lot."

"Not *that* kinda ride. How about a nice, evening horseback ride?"

I feel myself relaxing at just the thought. "You always know exactly what I need. Let me just put the girls in the house, then we can get the horses ready."

We head into the barn, and after we get the horses ready, I help Mel mount her horse. Once I've mounted mine, we head out toward the riding area side by side.

I glance over, and Mel looks so peaceful, not to mention sexy. Our horses keep pace with each other as we circle the area. We stop at the gate and dismount, then close the gate behind us so the horses can exercise at their own pace. Mel's leaning on the fence watching them.

"I'm so glad you wanted to do this," I say.

"We both needed it. I love watching them run."

"Me too. They truly are majestic beings."

"They sure are."

We let the horses run for a little longer, then we walk them back to the stables. We give them each a small treat after we take their equipment off. We pet each of them for a few minutes before we head inside.

"We need to do that more often," I say.

"I agree."

"How about now we do another season of *Nine-Nine*?"

"Oh my god, you're addicted."

"Thanks to you!"

After plowing through another season, we head off to bed.

The rest of the week is pretty much the same. Mel won't stop teasing me about having a man crush on Jake Peralta. What can I say? He's a funny dude.

Friday night rolls around, and we decide to indulge in a gooey extra cheese and pepperoni pizza and more *Brooklyn Nine-Nine.*

"You ready for tomorrow night?" I ask.

"Yeah. I know it sounds strange, but I'm actually looking forward to it. I'm picking Tammy up around ten for our beauty appointment."

"I'm glad you're gonna get that done, but trust me when I say, you're a stunner without it."

"Flattery will get you everywhere, my love."

"As long as it gets me in your pants."

"You wouldn't fit in my pants, silly," she says with a snort-laugh.

"Funny, funny, funny."

"Why, thank you," she says with a curtsy.

Mel's cell rings, and I hear her say, "Hey, Jay" when she answers.

"He wants to talk to you," she says, handing the phone to me.

"Hey, man. What's up?" I say.

"Since the ladies will be at the salon in the morning, I thought we could go together and grab our tuxes."

"That works."

"Okay. Tell Mel I'll pick Tammy up and drop her at your house, then we can head down to the men's shop after they leave."

"Great. I'll see you in the morning."

After I fill Mel in on the plan change, we head off to bed, both of us exhausted from a busy week.

If only she knew part of my exhaustion was not sleeping well. I'm still so torn about Aunt Mimi that I haven't had a good night's sleep since the day I agreed to keep her secret. I've almost told Mel countless times, but I couldn't do it. All I can see is the pleading in her aunt's eyes begging me not to break her niece's heart.

But what about when she loses her battle? How the hell am I gonna get Mel through it? And will she forgive me for keeping this secret? Maybe I need to talk to Aunt Mimi again.

I manage to get a few hours of restless sleep, and I'm awakened way too early by a very chipper woman and two crazy dogs. I get my shit together and head out to join Mel for a light breakfast and coffee out on the back patio. I hear a car pull into the driveway, and the dogs run to the fence, barking like crazy.

"Hey, Mel!" I hear Jay yell.

"We're back here!" I shout.

Jay and Tammy head our way, and the ladies get ready to leave. Once I hear Mel's car pull out, I say, "I have to make a couple quick stops, if you don't mind."

"Of course not."

"I'm getting Mel a tiara to wear tonight. After I pick it up, I wanna drop it at the salon as a surprise."

"Mind if I copy that idea for Tammy?"

"Not at all. So hey, what's the deal with you two?"

"I wish I knew. I really like her, man, but I can't get through."

"That's rough. It took some time with Mel, but we got there."

"Yeah. I hope it works out for me and Tammy."

After we finish up at the jewelers, we head over to the salon.

"I don't see the girls," I say.

We head inside and stop at reception.

"May I help you gentlemen?"

"We're dropping something off for our girlfriends, Mel and Tammy."

"They're in the back getting shampooed."

"Great. Then we can surprise them. Can you ask whoever does their hair to make it work with these?" I say.

"May I?" the receptionist asks.

"Of course."

She opens the boxes, and her jaw drops. "Wow. They're very lucky ladies."

"We're the lucky ones," Jay says, and all the women within earshot sigh in unison.

The receptionist grabs sticky notes so we make sure the right tiara goes to the right woman. We sneak out before the girls come back out front.

A few minutes later, we pull into the parking lot at the men's store, walk in the door, and come face to face with Daniel the asshole.

"I didn't know you served losers in this store," Daniel says to the salesman helping him. Not wanting to cause a scene, Jay and I walk to the other side of the store and wait for someone to help us. Of course, the dickhead can't just let us be.

"Picking up tuxes for tonight? I'm looking forward to seeing the dumb blonde get what's coming to her."

"Don't start," I warn.

Daniel ignores me and turns to Jay. "And why are you wasting money on a tux? Your blow-up wearing a fancy dress?"

"Shut the fuck up," Jay says in a low growl.

"Make me," Daniel says.

Jay and I both laugh and walk away again. "He sounds like a spoiled brat," Jay says.

"Yeah. But a damn lucky one. I really wanted to deck him again. If there's one thing Mel isn't, it's dumb."

"Quite the opposite. I just hope that little punk gets his some day."

"Me too."

After we get our tuxes, we head back home to wait for the girls. I grab a couple of tennis balls out and toss them to the dogs. They run, chasing each other, while Jay and I talk.

"So, man, any tips on how I can get through to Tammy?"

"I hate to say patience because I know better than anyone how hard that is. But if I'd pushed Mel too hard, I think I woulda pushed her away."

"I know. And that's the last thing I want with Tammy. So, I guess I'll have to settle for being friends for now."

"Look at this way. She did agree to be your date tonight. That's gotta be something."

"It is, but I can't tell you how times I've wanted to grab her and kiss her."

"Trust me, I get it. I had to resist that more times than I care to remember. But, man, the first time, it was beyond anything I could have imagined."

Jay nods but doesn't say anything else.

We're sitting out back enjoying some beer when I hear Mel's car pull in. My chin hits the ground when I see them come out back.

Chapter Twenty-Four

Mel

Tammy and I walk into the hair salon, and it's busy. No surprise on a Saturday. The receptionist greets us and takes us to the shampoo area. Tammy and I sit back to back waiting for the shampoo girl to finish with another customer.

After we're both done being shampooed, they take us out to the front and seat us next to each other. The receptionist walks over to our hairdressers with two felt boxes.

"Two handsome gentlemen stopped by and dropped these off. Which of you is Mel?"

"That's me," I say. She hands me one box and hands the other to Tammy. We both open them at the same time. We look at each other, eyes wide, when we see a tiara in each box.

"Oh my god, those two," Tammy says.

"They're the best," I say.

"We were instructed to do your hair in a way that would work with the tiaras, so we were thinking a braid for you, Mel, and an up-do for you, Tammy."

"I'm good with mine," I say.

"Me too," Tammy says.

After they finish our hair and put the tiaras in place, they take us to the makeup and nail area. While I get my makeup done, Tammy gets a manicure, then we switch.

After we're done with our pampering, we head back to my house where Jay's waiting with Judd. I pull into the garage and park, then Tammy and I head to the backyard.

"Holy shit! Two princesses just walked into the backyard," Judd says when he sees us.

Jay stands next to Judd and bows to us. We hear a couple of whistles and see Damien and Lexi standing at the fence.

"Damn, you two look even more amazing than usual," Lexi says.

"At the risk of getting in trouble with my wife, I agree," Damien adds.

Suddenly feeling self-conscious as my face heats up, I stare at my feet. Glancing over at Tammy, she's doing the same thing.

"Uh-uh," Judd scolds. "I want those heads held high. Especially tonight when we walk into that ballroom."

We both nod and take a seat at the patio table. Jay and Judd join us after Damien and Lexi head home. Once the men finish their beers, Jay and Tammy get ready to head out.

"The limo will be by around six-thirty," I say.

I sit down on the couch, and Judd joins me until it's time for him to shower. When he comes out, I'm dressed. In all his naked glory, Judd walks over to me and looks me up and down.

"My god, you're the most stunning woman I've ever seen."

"Why, thank you, handsome. Especially for this," I say pointing at my tiara.

"I get a feeling tonight's gonna be a good night," Judd says.

"Me too."

While Judd's getting dressed, I take the dogs out to the backyard. I can feel eyes on me, and when I turn around, he's standing there gawking at my back.

He joins me outside and says, "I love the way that braid is pointing at your sexy little ass. I cannot wait to get you out of that dress later."

Lexi comes over to get the girls. Once they're in Damien and Lexi's yard, I hand her the bag with their stuff. We head back inside just as the limo pulls up.

After the driver picks up Jay and Tammy, he drives us to the Imperial Ballrooms in Lancaster. Our event is being held in the fanciest of all the rooms, The Imperial Grande Ballroom.

The room lives up to its name in every way. But not one thing in that room is more attractive than my Judd. Heads turn when the four of us walk in, most of them with smiles across their faces. But there are three people standing near the main table with the biggest scowls on their faces.

"Wish I could say I was surprised to see them," I say nodding toward Abby, Daniel, and Trish. Before I get a chance to say anything else, Allie comes running over, Dane in tow.

"Oh my god, you look amazing. I love the tiara," Allie gushes. "And, Tammy, oh my god, you're stunning."

"Thank you," Tammy says shyly.

"Thanks, Allie. For everything," I say.

"We have a table held, if you'd like to sit with us," Allie says.

"Of course," I say. The six of us walk over to the table and do some people-watching.

Of course, no matter where we go, the three grump-kateers sneer at us. Unwilling to take the high road, they make their way to our table.

"Well, well, if it isn't the loser table," Trish spits.

"Seriously, Trish, just leave us the hell alone," I say. "This shit is really old at this point, and I'm sick and damn tired of dealing with you."

"Awww, poor princess," Trish says.

"So, is that it? You're jealous?" Tammy asks.

"Of that loser? Never," Trish says.

"Well, you sure sound like it to me," Tammy says.

Trish sticks her nose up in the air, sniffs, and storms back to Daniel.

"I gotta tell ya, I don't know how you survived growing up with her," Tammy says.

"Me either." *You don't know the half of it and the shit she put me through.*

We're standing by our table when we see Mr. O'Laughlin and his wife headed our way.

"Good evening," he says.

"Good evening, sir," I say.

"Greetings, sir," Jay says.

"You two no longer need to call me sir, not that you ever did. Honey, I'd like you to meet two of my recently-retired and top executives. Forgive me, this is my wife, Joyce."

"A pleasure to meet you," I say. "I couldn't have asked for a better boss than your husband."

"I second that," Jay says.

"I've heard a lot of positive things about both of you over the years. I was a bit surprised to hear you'd both retired, but I understand," Joyce says.

"I do, too. And I'm sorry it came to that, but things always have a way of working out," Mr. O'Laughlin says. "If you'll excuse us, we need to make the rounds.

We all look at each other, puzzled. "What the heck was that all about?" I ask.

"Your guess is as good as mine," Jay says.

We turn to look at Allie, and she shrugs her shoulders. After a delicious dinner of filet mignon and lobster tail, Mr. O'Laughlin walks to the podium at the front of the ballroom.

"Welcome to our annual retirement celebration," Mr. O'Laughlin says. "We have two honorees tonight. I'd like to ask Jason Donnelly and Melissa McNeill to please come up."

"Did you know about this?" I ask Judd.

"I did. Allie gave me a heads up, but I was sworn to secrecy."

Jay holds out his arm. I link mine through his, and we approach the podium. I take a quick glance over at the terrible threesome, and they do not look happy. I laugh to myself as Jay and I reach the podium.

"These two amazing employees started their employment together, both of them as part of our college intern program. I was so impressed with their skills that I hired each of them. Throughout their career, Jason in IT, and Melissa in Finance, they worked their way to my executive board, and I could not have been more pleased by their performance. To that end, I was saddened to hear of their intention to retire, and after some investigation, I discovered the reason."

I look at Jay and he gives me the slightest shake of his head, as Mr O'Laughlin continues. "As a small token of my gratitude, I'd like to present each of them with a gift. First, Melissa is being presented with a pair of two-carat diamond earrings. Second, Jason is being presented with a genuine Rolex watch. I'd like to invite each of them to say a few words."

"Ladies first," Jay says.

I step up to the podium. "Thank you, Mr. O'Laughlin, for this incredible honor. More importantly, thank you for guiding me through a fulfilling career. You never once made me feel like I was any less, or that I had to try harder because I'm female. I also owe a huge debt of gratitude to Jason and Allie for being amazing co-workers," I say.

I step aside and Jay takes his turn. "Like Melissa, I need to give a huge thank you to Mr. O'Laughlin for the opportunity. Despite being stuck with this troublemaker for over twenty years," Jay nods my way, "working for you was a pleasant experience." Laughter fills the room while I scowl at Jay before I join in the laughter. "I'm looking forward to the next chapter in my life, though I have no idea what that will be." After his remarks, Mr. O'Laughlin returns to the podium.

"And now, I have one final gift for the two of you." I see men in suits move in front of each of the ballroom's exits.

What the hell is going on?

Mr. O'Laughlin continues. "After a three-month long investigation by several government agencies, it was brought to my attention that my nephew, Daniel, was using my company as his own personal playground. His antics almost cost me everything. Daniel is being charged with embezzlement, racketeering, and a host of other charges. Abigail Donaldson is being charged with fraud. Daniel hired her to alter financial reports. The two of them were plotting to frame Ms. McNeill. And because of their dislike of Ms. McNeill, they also attempted to harass Mr. Donnelly into quitting. More important than that, however, is the apology I owe Melissa and Jason. Daniel treated them horribly and left them with no option but to retire."

I stand there with my mouth hanging open. Even hearing Mr. O'Laughlin's words still has me thinking I'm dreaming.

But I'm not.

Mr O'Laughlin motions his hand toward Daniel's table. I look over and see two men in suits approach the table. Jay and I stand there watching in disbelief as we see Daniel and Abby being handcuffed and led out of the ballroom.

"What the fuck just happened?" Jay whispers in my ear.

"I'm as stunned as you are, my friend," I whisper back.

Jay and I make our way back to our table.

"Well, Allie didn't tell me about *that,*" Judd says.

"I sure as hell didn't know," Allie says.

"I'm still trying to process what just happened," I say.

"Me too," Jay adds.

I look up when I see Trish slink over. I don't even try to fight off a smirk. "I came here with Daniel," Trish says.

"And?" I make sure my voice portrays that I really don't care.

"Well, I need a ride home."

"Again, and?"

"I'm your sister. Give me a ride."

"Call a damn ride share."

"Are you kidding? That costs money."

"Not my problem."

"That's how you treat family?"

"Let me tell you something." I gesture my hand around the group standing behind me. "This is my family."

"Not one of them's a blood relative."

"Your point?"

Trish glares. She grits her teeth. "I'm family. They're not."

"You know what you are to me? You're my mother's other daughter. Nothing more. You've treated me like shit as far back as I can remember. And I'm beyond damn tired of it."

"What if Daniel needs bail money and wants me to pay?"

"Then get some money."

"You know I don't have money."

"Then get a damn job. We've already had this discussion."

"So, you won't even let me ride home with you?"

"Hell no. Have a great rest of your night. I sure as hell will."

"Bitch," Trish says as she stomps off.

"She's unbelievable," I say, shaking my head.

"She sure is," Judd says.

We start to get ready to head out when Mr. O'Laughlin walks over. "Is there any chance I can convince you two to unretire?" he asks Jay and I.

"I can only speak for myself, but I'll have to decline. I loved my job with you, but I've found something I love just as much," I say.

"I understand. At least allow me to fund it then, as part of your retirement gift."

"That's very generous, but how about a compromise? I'm all set as far as funding the business, but I know an organization that could use the help."

"Tell me more."

"Monday morning, I have a meeting with Meals on Wheels to start donating meals and time to them. The woman I spoke with on the phone told me they're struggling to get donations."

"Then, please allow me. I'm going to write a check to them as my gift to you."

"Thank you, sir."

"My pleasure. And, Jay, what about you?"

"At the moment, I'm just relaxing."

"Then, I'll give you a check in the same amount, and you can decide how you wish to use it. That is, unless you want to come back."

"I appreciate that, but like Mel, I'm good where I am."

Mr. O'Laughlin pulls his checkbook out of the inner pocket on his jacket and writes a check for each of us.

I immediately tuck it into my handbag without looking at the amount. "Thank you so much. For everything," I say.

"Thank you for being such top-notch employees."

We all nod and head outside where the limo waits for us. After hugging Allie and Dane goodbye, we get into the limo. "Well, that was interesting," I say.

"Talk about an understatement," Jay says.

"In my wildest dreams, I could not have imagined something like that," I say.

I notice Judd doesn't say anything for the ride home. After the limo drops us off, we go sit out back. "You okay?" I ask.

"Yeah, just trying to process everything."

"Yeah."

"You can ask me," he says after a few moments.

"Ask you what?" I know exactly what he means.

"I'm glad Abby got arrested. At least she'll be out of our lives."

I nod. "I didn't wanna upset you."

"Thanks. Since Damien and Lexi said they'd keep the dogs overnight, how about we head inside? I'm exhausted after everything that happened."

"Okay."

The next morning, we take our breakfast out to the back patio. I hear a couple of dogs going crazy. I look over and see both of our girls at the fence. Judd and I walk over.

"So, how was last night?" Lexi asks.

"You won't believe what happened," I say. I fill Lexi and Damien in on the whole sordid story.

"Holy hell, that's crazy," Lexi says.

"For sure. And then Trish comes over thinking I'll feel sorry for her. She actually asked for a ride and bail money for Daniel."

"Talk about batshit crazy."

"Totally. Otherwise, though, we had a nice time."

"Glad to hear it."

After a quiet weekend attempting to recover from Friday night's events, I head down to the Meals for Wheels office while Judd heads to

the farmer's market to man the booth. While I'm there, I present the check that Mr. O'Laughlin gave me.

The woman I'm meeting with, Diana, looks at the check and her jaw drops. "Are you sure this is all for us?" she asks in disbelief.

"Yes, ma'am. As part of my retirement gift, the CEO of the company gave me a quarter of a million dollars to donate to the charity of my choice."

"You have no idea what this will mean for us."

"It's my pleasure. This cause is so important, and I'm happy to support it in any way I can. What do you need as far as meal deliveries?"

"We already have a staff who prepares meals, so we'll just need to schedule your delivery shift. We have an opening on Sunday, if that works."

"That's perfect."

"Great, let's get you signed up. Can you start this coming Sunday?"

"Yes, ma'am."

After we complete the necessary paperwork, I head to the market where Judd's completely swamped and starting to get frazzled. I jump in and get things under control, and when we get a lull, he plops down in one of the chairs.

"Is this getting to be too much?" I ask.

"Sometimes."

"I agree. I really need to hire someone to do this."

"Yeah. Look, we only have a few more weeks left before we close for the season. I can hang in there if you can."

"I can, and we'll make sure we have someone reliable for next year."

"Deal."

Judd and Mel's story concludes in *Into the Sunset,* coming December 2023.

Acknowledgments

Proofread and edited by Melony Carter-Alexander

* * *

Cover by Carter Cover Designs

About the Author

Samantha Michaels was born in 1973 in the small town of Abington, PA and was raised and still lives in Hatboro, PA (both suburbs of Philadelphia). She is married to her high school sweetheart and they have a rescue dog, a beautiful Black Lab named Holly.

When she's not writing or working at her full-time job, she enjoys watching her Philly sports team (hopefully) win, listening to heavy metal/hard rock music, Texas Hold Em, reading, and spending time with friends and family.

Her love of reading began at a young age, thanks to her mother and Sesame Street. Her mom read to her constantly, and by three years old, she was reading on her own, and hasn't stopped. This eventually turned into a love of writing.

To learn more:
Website
Newsletter

Also by
Samantha Michaels